EMOTIONALLY POWERFUL

First Edition
Published by Fairies and Fantasy Pty Ltd 2019
Paperback ISBN: 978-0-6485427-8-0
Hardcover ISBN: 978-1-922390-14-1

www.selinafenech.com

EMOTIONALLY POWERFUL

THE EMPATH 3 CHRONICLES

SELINA A. FENECH

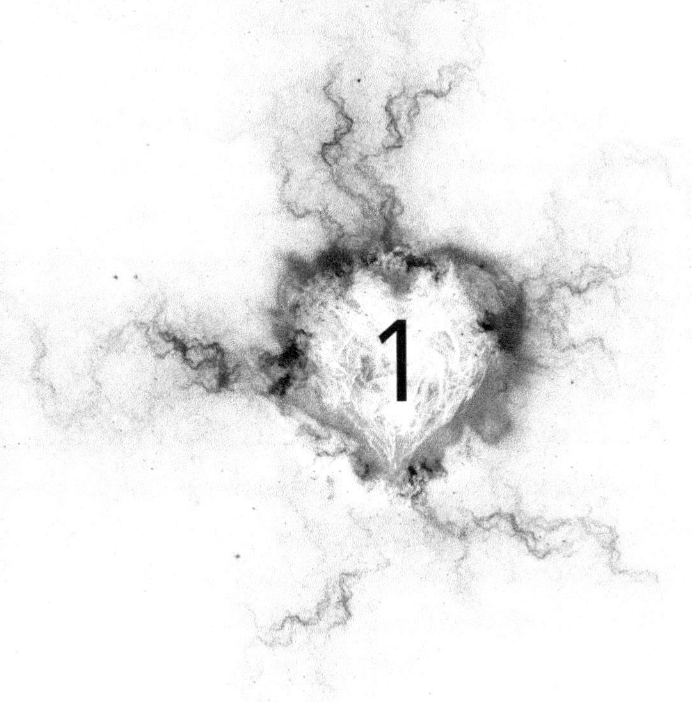

The elevator dinged beside us, but I didn't want to separate my lips from Dean's.

My body felt light and giddy after having just emptied myself of the other powers I had drained. Yet the world felt so full now, of new possibilities. Of romance. I could taste the salt of Dean's tears and the sweetness of his tongue and didn't care that half of Limbus stared at us from down the corridor. Dean and I embraced each other with needy arms, living only for this kiss that we had been denied for so long.

Dean slowed down first, drawing back softly. I didn't ever want the moment to end, but then he did something that filled my heart even more.

He pressed his temple against mine, and whispered into my ear, "I love you."

I didn't even have to think. The words shot up from my very heart itself. "I love you too."

Dean squeezed me around the waist and kissed my cheek slowly. "Everything will be different now. Everything will be amazing."

My eyes were on Dean, his shallow breaths, his purple lips, his closed eyelids.

His hand was cold and still in mine.

Machines helped him breathe, monitored all his vital functions, pumped nutrients and fluids into his body that couldn't support its own needs. They whirled and beeped, matched by others around the Limbus ward, the only sound in the room.

It had been more than a week since the leech had got to Dean. A week of sleepless nightmares and unstoppable tears.

I squeezed Dean's hand. I had dragged him into this life, the world of empaths. This was my fault. *All my fault.*

The moment I found Dean at the train station still felt like a dream, or a nightmare. I had slumped, curled up beside

Dean's lifeless form on the platform concrete. The agents close by had arrived, then the Crossmans came, and my parents, and everyone tried to console me, tell me it was going to be okay, but I was lost.

My chest was tight with heartbreak; I wanted, *needed,* to be with him. His body was here, but I knew he wasn't. Not the real Dean.

"Hi Livvy. Back again, I see." One of the nurses pushed the curtain aside and smiled at me with pitying eyes.

"Every day," I replied, trying to force a grin.

Limbus had been good about letting me come in and see Dean whenever I wanted. They knew I needed to be here. I couldn't tear myself away from him. It was too soon. I felt guilty every time I went home, but I also knew there was no chance Dean would spontaneously wake up on his own. My parents had been understanding too, but I knew it wouldn't last forever. Eventually I would have to join the land of the living again.

Kimmy followed the nurse over and jumped up onto the end of the bed. She walked up to nuzzle a soft nose-kiss for Dean and me, then curled up into a black and white purring ball beside Dean's tucked in legs.

The nurse took readings and jotted down some notes on a tablet screen with a stylus. "Just normal checks."

"Any changes since yesterday?" I asked, already knowing the answer.

She patted her hand on my shoulder. "No, sweetie. But as soon as there are, you'll be the first person I tell. I promise."

I nodded and waited for her to leave the area again. There would be no changes, no life returned to Dean, until the leech was brought down and brought in. And Limbus seemed no closer to achieving that.

I tiptoed to gently pull the curtain that surrounded Dean's bed closed again. I didn't know why I moved so quietly. It wasn't like my noise was going to wake anyone. Moving back to my chair, it felt like a strong current blew through my head, bringing a weird sense of detachment with it. My vision blurred. I grasped the chair back with one hand, holding tightly to my forehead with the other.

The feeling dissipated just as quickly as it started and I blinked, looking around. *Weird.*

Sitting, I put my legs up, resting them on the edge of Dean's bed and holding his hand. I spoke, not because I thought he could hear, but because I needed to imagine him with me.

"Let's see. What do I have to tell you today? I slept in your bed again last night. Although it's starting to not smell like you already. Mom and Dad are missing you too. Dad keeps cooking more for dinner than we need, forgetting he doesn't have a teenage boy to feed anymore."

Tapping my fingers on Dean's hand, I stared at his pale face. He was still Dean, but the stillness of his body made him look like he was made out of wax. I kept imagining him opening his eyes, stretching his arms, and yawning, like he was just waking from a nap. And every time I imagined it, my eyes filled with tears.

"So anyway," I said, clearing my throat, "I've got training this afternoon. I figure it will be good for me, but it will be hard without you there. I hate the feeling I'm going back to my life, without you. It makes me feel like I'm giving up on you. But it's not helping anyone, sitting in here moping either. The longer I do this, the longer you'll be out. The only way to save you is to find and capture the leech. I need to help. I want to be the hero that saves you."

The word hero made me laugh at myself. I've been such a superhero, sitting in here, crying and holding my valiant hero's hand while he lay helpless in bed.

I couldn't keep waiting for Limbus to fix this. They didn't seem to have any leads. The leech was either way too lucky or way too clever for them.

But I had a shot. The leech knew my face. Knew what I

could do. He'd gone after Dean right after he saw us. He'd felt … familiar.

And the fact Dean hadn't used his panic button must have meant the leech didn't seem like a threat to Dean until too late. Maybe it was someone we knew.

That was something I could work with. I'd drained people before; I'd restored people before. I would find the leech, and take everything he'd stolen from the others, even if it made me explode, and I'd put all those powers back where they belonged.

After I'd restored him to his body, Jake had told his parents he hadn't been aware of anything at all, of any time passing or any feelings or thoughts during the time I had drained him and held his powers inside me. I wondered if Dean was the same. He was a blocker, which had to be a bit different. I had only given the power back to proesthians like me. I didn't even know if I could give back a blocker's powers. But I couldn't think about it at that moment. I couldn't dare imagine not succeeding. Last time I did, I cried so hard I vomited in the sink.

I pulled Dean's hand to my lips and kissed the back of it. "I promise, one way or another, I'll get you back." I looked around the room, at all the leech's victims. "I'll get every single one of you back."

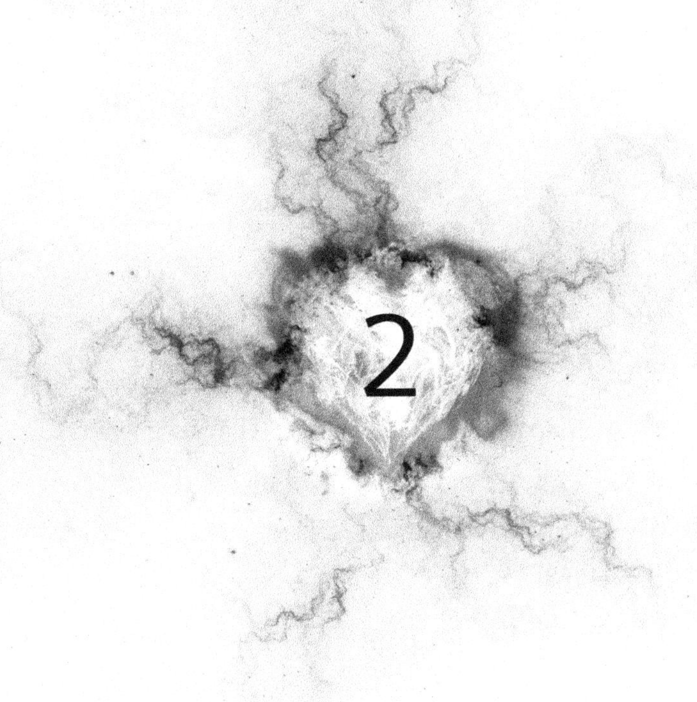

2

The Crossmans looked more nervous with every passing day. Dean hadn't managed to restore their powers that night, before he was drained. From what I'd heard, he was really close, but close wasn't what they needed. They were anxious about the leech, and being powerless left them relying entirely on the other Limbus agents.

I noticed one day they had both started to carry concealed firearms. It felt like everyone was waiting to hear the news the leech had struck again with every passing hour. But after Dean, everything had gone quiet.

Limbus had ramped up training for us younger empaths.

Our teachers had begun introducing a lot more aggressive self-defense into what had been mostly meditation and focus classes before. They probably wanted us to have some chance of defending ourselves, or at least the illusion that we could.

I didn't fear the leech anymore. My fear had been replaced with pure hatred. An anger so deep that it changed me. I could tell from the way my parents looked at me that it wasn't necessarily for the better. I let that anger burn deep, as though it was the fuel that I needed to keep going.

Security overall had been increased both at Limbus and within our household, and the times Mom and Dad allowed me to catch the train I always had at least one agent with me. Mostly, Limbus drove me anywhere I needed to go.

Home was the only place I didn't have a full escort. I hadn't been to school. My parents let me take sick days. I missed Nati, but how could I explain any of this to her?

When I walked into the gym, the room was quiet, but there was a whisper of excitement from some of the younger kids. They watched Felix, who stood beside a metal trolley with plastic crates stacked on top, twiddling his goatee. Bastian, Emma, and Sway were in the middle of the room, sitting beside each other, cross-legged with their eyes closed. Rayni was with the few other younger kids, who I now knew were Ada, Cam, and Max. She seemed a bit brighter than she had for a while. I couldn't see color auras anymore, but could still sense sadness in her underneath her smile.

My eyes still felt raw and my mouth was fixed downwards. How long would it take after Dean's draining for me to be able to put on a brave face like that?

For now, all my energy went into training. It was essential in order for me to grow physically and mentally stronger. I needed anything I could get if I was going to start hunting down the leech. Of course, I hadn't divulged that plan to the Crossmans, but I was sure they suspected. They knew where I was and how angry I had become, even without empath senses.

The Crossmans were deep in conversation together, checking things on their tablet screens, before Mr. Crossman spoke loudly, addressing the room. "All right, everyone, gather around. Felix has brought something for you all."

Everyone came closer, and Felix reached into one of the boxes. So that was where all of the excitement was stemming from. Some of the kids must have already known what was happening in training today.

"You get a superhero suit, and you get a superhero suit!" Felix cried, as he pulled black jumpsuits out of the box and chucked them into waiting hands.

One landed in my grasp, and I rubbed the thick, silky fabric between my fingers. I glanced over at one of the uniformed agents in black standing guard near a door. It looked almost the same as what they wore. My eyebrows went up.

A rush of chatter filled the room. The younger kids were so excited their emotions were flooding over. It was like a domino effect, catching to every empath in the group. Even I managed a wry half-smile.

Felix clapped his hands together. "Okay, I know you are all dying to play dress-up, but I need to explain the suit to you first so you don't rip holes in these things, because they aren't cheap." He dashed out of the room briefly then came back in, pushing a mannequin wearing one of the suits. Felix rolled the mannequin to the front of the group and stood beside it. "These are the same kinds of suits that the grown-up operatives wear, just scaled down for you guys. With a shrink ray!"

Everyone oohed and awed.

"Not actually with a shrink ray." Dr. Crossman clarified dryly. "These suits have a lot of features that can help an empath utilize their powers, or help with things an empath's powers can't. You kids are very talented, but sometimes that isn't all there is to it. Strength, speed, and toughness can't solve every problem you are going to face. From now on, you'll be wearing these during training sessions to learn their features and get used to them, just like our adult operatives."

Felix pointed to the different features of the suit as he went, starting with the soap-bar-sized flat section near the wrist. "Capacitive-touch smart-screen that—once fully activated—links up to the Limbus system, GPS, telecom systems, vitals monitoring, and more. Plus, it has pretty heart-shaped notification lights! That was my design choice. Utility belt contains various tools for covert operations and survival in many conditions, including tasty ration packs. You don't get those yet either. The fabric has bio-electric protection, and is blade- and bullet-proof."

I ran my hands over the soft fabric again. As the material moved, the light caught on small metal fibers running through. The suits sounded pretty impressive. I doubted they were leech-proof though.

Felix went on and on, explaining every single device, then let the excited group split up to go and try the suits on.

I made my way towards the bathrooms in the corner of the gym, then noticed Emma heading that way too. She locked eyes with me, and we stopped. She bit her lip, then opened her mouth as though she was about to say something.

I spun on my heel, heading out to the bathrooms down the hall. I wasn't in the mood to interact with her. I fumed, imagining she was happy, that in her mind Dean deserved what he got. Or even worse, imagining having her pity us.

I hated that Emma had been getting the full team experience the whole time I'd been mourning Dean. I'd been hearing glowing reports of how well she'd been doing. How clever and talented she was. Emma had even officially been let off 'house arrest' at Limbus. Not that it meant anything right then. She, Sway, Rayni, Bastian and the others who lived at the agency were pretty much on lockdown, unable to go out in town without extra permissions and security.

I closed myself into a toilet stall, despite having the whole bathroom block to myself. I undressed and then pulled the suit on, one foot at a time. It looked far too small at first, but slipped on snuggly and smoothly. The black material was like spandex or Lycra, but it was far lighter with a subtle scale-like texture, and a thicker vest area. I zipped up the front and stepped out. As I pulled my hair back in a ponytail I looked into the mirror.

The old me would have been giggling with excitement. I looked like a superhero. But the new me had red-rimmed eyes with dark purple smudges beneath them, and a hard grimace.

Part of me wished I could feel that innocent giddiness again. Maybe one day it would come back. I didn't want this serious girl in the mirror to be the permanent version of myself. But I needed her right now.

Back inside the training room, the kids were being paired up to practice some karate-based self-defense moves to experience the full range of movement the suit provided. Bastian and Emma paired together as normal and were already suited up and sparring.

Bastian had pulled his brown ringlets into a puffy top-knot. He shook his head at Emma and slapped his forearm. "No. I know you can do better than that. You know it too. Don't worry about the external. You've got what you need inside. Go again."

Emma nodded, moving through the stances a second time to strike a blow that made Bastian laugh and clap. She pushed her red hair back over her ear, exposing her clear eyes, the natural pink to her cheeks. *Huh.* She wasn't wearing any make-up.

Sway walked up next to me, wrinkling her nose and tugging at the fabric around her non-existent hips. "I guess this is better than scrubs."

I looked at her petite, boy-like figure, and the shaved-side blonde pixie hair swirled on top of her head. "You look like a cartoon character. In a good way."

Sway smiled and her eyes glittered. When I didn't smile in

return, she followed my gaze to Emma and Bastian. "You two have some history, hey. She told me a bit about it."

I pursed my lips. I could only imagine what Emma had been telling everyone. Because I doubted any of it was the truth. I started some warm-up stretches and muttered, "I can't believe everyone thinks she's so great. How does she deserve this …?" *When Dean …* I gulped away a sob and firmed my expression.

Sway moved her face close to mine, inspecting me wide-eyed. "You really don't like her?"

"She's so … superficial and selfish." *Like I used to be.*

"Really? Wow. I haven't noticed. She's more of a thinky-thoughtful, tries-to-be-bestest-friends girl." Sway bent over beside me, stretching as well. Sway and Emma had been in rooms just down the hall from each other since moving into Limbus.

I imagined them bonding, up late chatting on each other's beds, and scowled. "Sounds like how I first saw Emma. Before I learned the truth."

"If it's worth anything, I think she's sorry." Bastian's voice startled me from my stretch. He'd come over beside us without me noticing. I bristled and stood up straight, but Emma hadn't followed him. She was over with the Crossmans.

"Emma's not what I expected either." Bastian shrugged his round shoulders. "She's actually a total egg-head under all that razzle dazzle. She's just spent so long pretending to be what she thought she had to be in order to be accepted, to survive."

A vivid memory of Emma's pre-cosmetic surgery photo flashed through my mind. She'd done so much to escape who she was. Maybe in the right, accepting environment, she could be the real her. And maybe the real her was nicer than I imagined.

I wasn't sure though. "Then why didn't you want to train with her? What did you see with your future vision that made you flip out when you met her?"

Bastian's brown cheeks glowed. "You know that elucidist powers don't always play out accurately."

Emma and Rayni came over before he could elaborate any further. They both held water bottles, and there was a vulnerability in Emma's smile I hadn't noticed before.

She tucked her hair behind an ear even though it hadn't fallen free, cleared her throat and said, "Hey, Livvy."

"Hey," I grunted. It was the first direct interaction we'd had since the comic convention and a tense silence built.

Bastian looked around at the four of us. "Wow, it's becoming a bit of a girls' club in here."

Sway scrunched up her lips in a pout. "I don't always feel like a girl, if that helps."

Emma tilted her head thoughtfully. "Are women more likely

to be empaths than men? Women are naturally more in tune with their emotions.”

Rayni's eyes lit up. “Actually, if you really look into it, that whole 'emotional women' and 'unemotional men' thing as a premise is nothing more than a sexist societal construct. Fairly damaging on the men's side too, making them bottle up their emotions—” Her eyes zipped over to me and her mouth clammed shut. I took a deep breath, my jaw twitching.

Sway beat her chest like a gorilla. “Crush the patriarchy, raaar!”

Bastian feigned terror. “I'm completely outnumbered!”

I snapped, “What? You're feeling put out because you're the only guy your age not lying in a coma?”

The smiles on everyone's faces dropped. Anger sizzled under my skin, and from the way Sway looked at me, I wondered if she could see my aura glowing red.

“Have you already forgotten about Dean? And Ash?”

The tremble of Rayni's bottom lip made me turn away. I bent to grab my water bottle from the mat then stalked off, filled with fury and shame.

Because for a moment, I had been enjoying myself too.

From behind my back I heard Emma tease Bastian. “Why didn't you see *that* coming?”

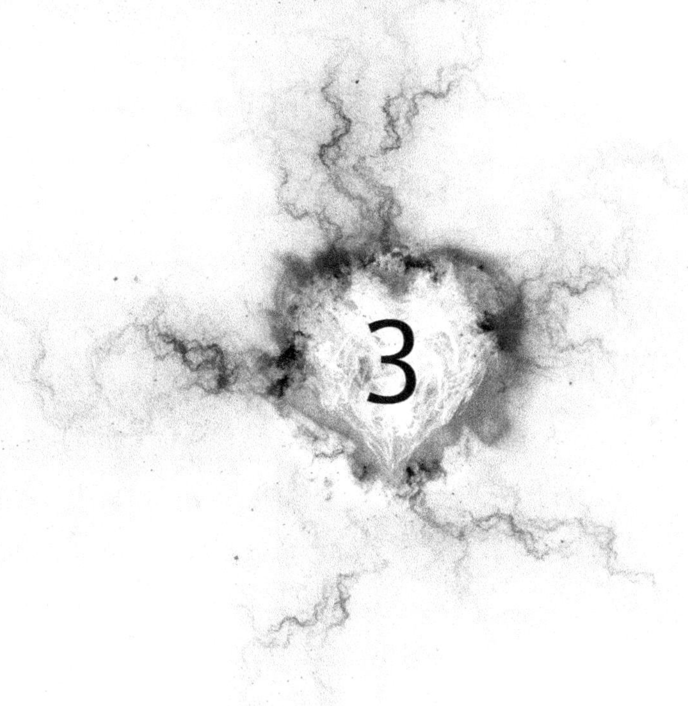

3

Dad had garlic and ginger sautéing in a pan, sizzling softly as he chopped vegetables. Mom sat next to me at the kitchen table, her fingers tapping away on her laptop keyboard, and she mumbled and muttered occasionally under her breath about insurance claim bureaucracy bull—her eyes would flash to me—*dirt.*

I had my head down on my folded arms, staring at the beads of condensation on my glass of water. Trying to do nothing, think of nothing. Another week had passed. I had started going to school again. I kept training. Nothing changed. Dean didn't wake up. The leech was still out there. I could have exploded from frustration. I wanted to rip the world apart, hunting for that monster. I wanted revenge and justice and to not feel all this hate all the time.

So I sat and did nothing and took slow, deep breaths.

I had kept up with my therapy sessions, out of a new office. Because the old office was at the institute, where all the buildings had been evacuated after the leech burned one to the ground. After he murdered Marigold.

My fists clenched, and my breathing was not slow and deep.

"This is almost ready. Can you set the table?" Dad called across the kitchen counter to us.

I started sliding my chair back, but Mom shut her laptop and smoothed her hand down my hair. "I'll do it." She stood up and kissed me on the top of the head, then went to the cupboard.

Plates clattered in her hand and she put them out around the table. I sat up so she could put one in front of me. "Thanks."

"No prob, bub," she said cheerily.

When she'd put three plates down, she still had one in her hand, hovering above the table. Her gaze flickered to me, then she took the plate back to the cupboard, probably hoping I hadn't noticed her slip-up. I wondered whether Dad was cooking too much food again. He'd started excusing it as 'making leftovers'. But it felt like he wanted to be sure, that just in case by some miracle Dean woke up perfectly fine and walked in the door, there'd be a meal for him here. I liked that idea too. But I knew it wouldn't happen.

Dad placed a huge serving bowl of stir-fry and one of rice into the middle of the table. Enough for us three and way more. *Bingo.*

"I'm glad you're here for dinner tonight. It feels like you've been at training or visiting Dean in all your spare hours," he said as he took his seat, "which is completely okay. But we've missed you."

"I've missed you both too." I smiled thinly, helping myself from the mountain of food. My stomach gurgled, hungry from the extra exercise and training. And below that I could feel my pull to Dean, that need to be close to him that lived deep in the pit of my being. "I want to be with Dean, too. I want to be there for him all the time like he was there for me. But it's not helpful. There was a point to him being by my side. It's actually kind of counterproductive for me to spend all of my time next to him. It won't wake him up."

Mom paused with the serving spoon in the rice. "Oh, Livvy-bear. We wish there was something we could do. We've racked our brains, and the Crossmans', on how we could help, but in this situation I'm afraid we're virtually useless."

I smiled, honestly and warmly. "You're far from useless. You help me so much just being here for me. I need you both to be my parents, and I'll handle the empath stuff."

Mom side-eyed Dad then, and I could tell they were edging around a conversation. She cleared her throat and put her cutlery down. "Livvy, you're not planning anything rash, right? We know you're determined to fix this, to save Dean, and we're worried you're going to try and do it alone."

After taking a deep breath, I sipped my water. It bugged me how they could always see straight through me. I appreciated that they cared, but I also knew I'd do anything I had to do to save Dean. *Anything.*

Unfortunately, so far, I had *nothing*. I didn't even have to lie. "I don't have any crazy plans."

Mom squinted at me like she really was trying to read my mind. "Because you're not alone, you know that, right? We all want to save Dean, and the others, and stop that criminal from hurting anyone else just as much as you want to. You have all of Limbus trying to help."

"And us," Dad added. "At least to keep doing the parent thing."

"Thanks, guys." I poked at my food, trying not to cry. "I love you."

"Right back at ya, Lollipop," Dad said with his mouth full.

Mom looked like she had something else to say when the doorbell rang.

Dad frowned. "I wonder who that could be. You expecting anyone?"

Mom shook her head. "Nope."

I scoffed at the tiny spark of foolish hope, imagining it really was Dean there, miraculously woken and come home for dinner.

Still, I sat frozen in place as Dad went to answer the door. *Limbus could have done it,* the hope reasoned. *Caught the leech, restored everyone. It could happen at any moment.*

Dad greeted someone happily, and I could hear his and another man's laughter.

"That's brilliant news. Come in! You have time for a beer?" Dad returned to the kitchen, followed by Terry. "You'll never guess who got promoted again!"

Mom hopped up and greeted him with a hug. "So soon? That's amazing! Congratulations."

Terry flashed his million-dollar smile. He wasn't in uniform, just wore jeans and a tucked-in polo shirt, but he still had that authoritarian police presence he always had.

I forced a smile. He wasn't my favorite person. "Hi Terry," I said, without getting out of my seat.

"Olivia, not getting into any new adventures?" He walked

past and patted me on the back, then took the empty chair across the table from me. He watched me with sparkling eyes. I worked hard not to roll mine.

Dad grabbed two beers from the fridge. "You're welcome to some dinner too; we've got plenty."

"If you insist." He grinned, taking a bottle from Dad and popping the top off.

Mom set a plate and silverware in front of him. She took her seat again and raised her water glass. "To your promotion."

"To Captain Pence." Dad chinked his bottle to her glass and Terry joined them.

"Just honored to serve my town." His tone gave me an uneasy feeling, but I tried to ignore it. Terry had always been a good friend to my parents, no matter how much he creeped me out. He held out his bottle to me and I clinked my cup against it politely.

"It's not as safe a place as people believe," he mused, taking a swig of his beer. "A strong police force is important to keep everything in check. There are bad guys around every corner."

Mom chuckled nervously. "I'm sure it's not really that bad. Most *bad guys* are just people society has failed in some way."

"Even those kids who trashed your shop, Jolene? Thugs with no respect for anything or anyone—that's what they are.

Menaces to society that will only get worse unless they are locked up or put down."

Dad tutted and gave Terry a stern but friendly look. "You know how we feel about the death penalty in this house."

Terry smiled an apology, but a shiver ran down my spine. I could sense a rising mix of emotions, a humming jitteriness in Terry that set my teeth on edge.

He ate a mouthful then pointed his fork at me while he spoke. "Your parents are big softies, but if they saw what I saw every day, their minds would change. For example, just last night I saved a woman's life, down in Bellston Main. A drug addict had her at knife point, trying to shake her up for cash—maybe more."

Mom sucked in a loud breath and gave Terry a warning look, but he kept going.

"I was able to intervene because I've done what I've needed to do to be in a position of power. In the war of good and evil, you've got to consider the greater good. I did what I had to, to save her life, before something really bad could happen."

He paused as if I was supposed to say something back, but I could only stare, aghast and confused. His tone, whatever message he was trying to get across, was creeping me out more than he had ever done before.

"How about you, Olivia?" he asked.

"Huh?"

"You must be starting to think about what to do after high school. Ever thought of joining the force?"

I stared around the table, all eyes on me and a heavy awkwardness setting in. "Not really. I don't think I'm the crime-fighting kind of girl."

Dad coughed and cleared his throat.

Terry helped himself to seconds of the food, piling it up and scraping the serving plates clean. "Oh? I would have thought, after your recent experiences, you might have gained a certain appreciation for that side of the world."

I stiffened. Just how much had my parents told him? They looked as confused as I felt though. "And what side of the world exactly is that?"

"You know …" He laughed. "The helpers—those who are powerful enough to help the powerless. Police, EMTs, that sort of thing."

My shoulders dropped a little, relieved.

"Or people with abilities like ours. Empaths." He winked at me and I dropped my fork.

Cutlery clattered near Mom and Dad as well, but my eyes were fixed on Terry.

My jaw wobbled as I tried to find words to deny what I was, and shocked to find out what he was, but he talked over me.

"No point denying it anymore. You know, I was almost thrown off my suspicions about you when that bleach-haired punk in your class ended up being an empath too. I'd set up that little ceiling incident to force something out of you but ended up getting him instead."

"Getting … Ash?" My breathing became rapid and panic made my vision blurry.

Mom gasped. "Terry? What are you—"

"Eat your dinner and be quiet," he replied tersely.

Her mouth closed and she smiled softly, and she and Dad robotically ate their dinner.

I jumped to my feet, my chair falling to the ground behind me. My mind raced.

"Isn't it amazing? The things we can do." He grinned at me like we were best friends, and took another mouthful of his food. "Getting ahead in life, making a real difference. It's all about power. This power. As much of this power as you can get."

My whole body turned to ice and my legs nearly buckled.

It's him.

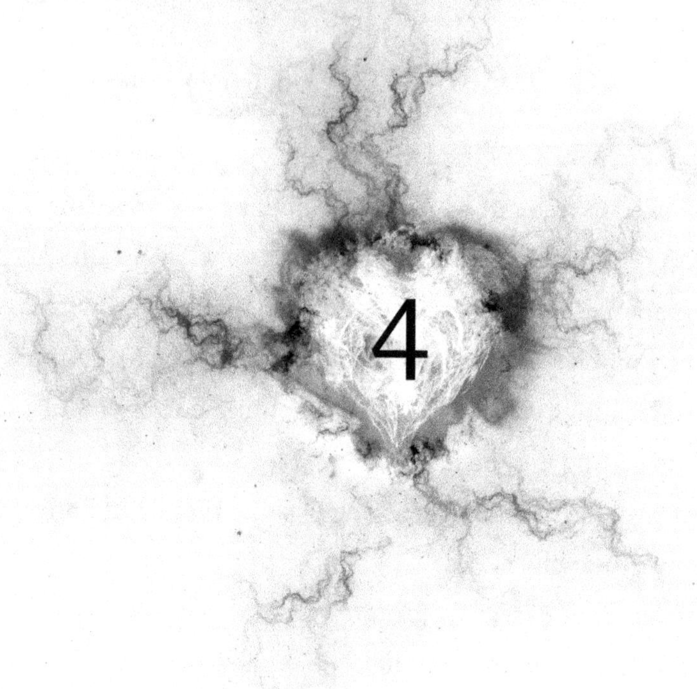

4

It's him. *Terry's the leech. He's sitting at dinner with my family, telling me he's the leech.*

I didn't know why. I didn't care what his motives were. I only knew I had to *stop him.*

I leaped straight over the tabletop and threw the hardest punch I could.

Everything spun around us, the wind from my movements sending napkins flying and plates crashing to the ground.

As my fist approached his cheek, he casually reached up and grabbed it.

It felt like I'd hit a block of steel. I cried out in agony as bones in my hand cracked.

He gave me a pitying look. "Olivia, please. I'm just here to tal—"

I swung my other fist, landing the uppercut under his chin. My punch glanced off him. He didn't even blink.

He snatched my second hand out of the air so fast I couldn't see it, and pushed against me.

My legs bent as he forced my back down onto the table with enormous strength.

Staring at me from above with menacing eyes, he grunted. "That was just rude, Olivia."

Plates crashed and clattered. My parents jolted into awareness. My mom cried out, and Dad heaved his chair back. "Let my daughter go right now."

Terry's mouth twitched and his eyes twinkled. He was drinking in their anger. They were only making him stronger. My chest flooded with sudden fear for my parents. I eyed the Limbus tracker bracelet, but Terry still held both my hands firmly.

He chuckled, like we'd just had a misunderstanding, but didn't let me go. "Now, now. Let's just put this all behind us, shall we?"

Mom bellowed, "Get out. Get out of my house!"

Terry sighed, and he flung me like a wet rag against the

wall. The plasterboard buckled beneath my impact and I crashed into a side table, falling down into a pile of smashed photo frames and broken ornaments. I saw stars. Punch-drunk, I flailed, tried to focus.

Terry stepped toward my terrified parents, waving his hands and chin in time as though conducting an orchestra. "My old friends. Come now, let's not fight."

I sobbed as my parents both smiled and nodded at him like puppets.

I squeezed both sides of the tracker with stinging fingers, preparing to set off the panic button. Terry shot me a smile and wrapped a hand around the back of my mom's neck, lifting her off the ground. I snatched my fingers away from the tracker before it flashed red.

"Stop!" I dragged myself up onto wobbly feet. I wanted to rush him, but I knew I wasn't as fast as he was. And Limbus's reaction to the panic button wouldn't be fast enough either. "Please, *please* don't hurt them. They aren't part of this."

"I really would hate to have to harm anyone. You won't make me, will you? No more sucker punches?"

I cradled my broken hands and nodded.

Terry put my mom back down on her feet, then brushed back his messed up blond hair with his hands, sighing. "I think

Jolene and Craig here are going to come for a ride with me."

A whimper escaped my mouth. "No, please don't."

Terry tilted his head to the side as though considering my plea. "You see, I am pretty sure your parents are *persons of interest* in a string of robberies downtown. I think it's best I take them into lockup. Just for a while. That should give you time to think about my offer."

"What offer?" I growled.

"To join forces, of course." He smiled, and it dripped with satisfaction. "I know what you did to those three boys. I know you're like me. You understand the scope of what people like us can *really* become. And with my help, you could be so much more."

My head shook and my lips twitched with overflowing hatred.

"Think about it," Terry snapped, *commanded*, and I felt the force of his command stronger than I'd ever felt Jake's power of suggestion. I forced it away only by the pure might of my anger.

Terry herded my parents toward the door. He stopped in front of me and picked a piece of broken glass from my shoulder. I whimpered as it slid free of my flesh. "But if you tell a soul about this, I can promise you right now, you'll never see your parents again."

With a million-dollar smile, he tapped the tip of my nose. "So, think on it long and hard, *Lollipop*. I know you'll make a good choice."

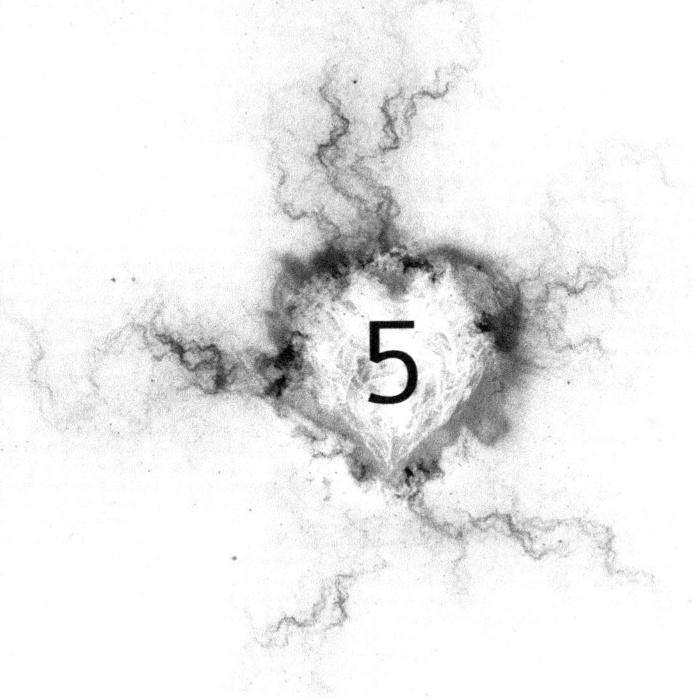

5

I didn't know how many hours I lay on the floor, curled in a ball. Aching all over, inside and out. Weeping. Choking on sobs.

It had been dark a long time before I could move again. My empath powers had worked to heal my physical injuries relatively quickly, at least enough to achieve basic functionality. I was sure parts of my hands were broken, and although I could move my fingers again, they still throbbed.

But it was nothing to the emotional pain that crippled me.

I should have pressed the panic button straight away. As soon as I suspected anything. Before he had any reason to threaten my parents. I could have played it cool, hidden it under the table, kept him talking.

I shouldn't have tried to take him on my own.

Coulda, shoulda, woulda etched repetitive patterns into my brain, scratching away my sanity.

My imagination tortured me, showing me Limbus arriving in time, the agents taking Terry down, bring him in, forcing him to restore those he'd drained. I had Dean back. Happy ending.

But instead, I had this.

Nothing.

Terry had taken everything from me.

I groaned and moved into a sitting position, my back against the wall. I angrily picked pieces of rice and glass off my clothes.

How did I miss this? I should have guessed it was him. The leech had felt so familiar, but I didn't connect that to Terry.

Not Terry, a pillar of our community. Not Terry, always there to help out. Not Terry, with his shining blond hair and winning smile. Terry, who deep down had always creeped me out, but I'd ignored that instinct because he was my parents' friend. Mr. Everyone Agrees He's A Great Man.

I stared at the tracker on my wrist. I could still press it. Still ask Limbus for help.

I needed help.

I was so wrong. I can't do this alone.

Tears started again, but I couldn't press the button. I'd seen firsthand what Terry was capable of. How he used people, used them up, discarded them. I didn't doubt for a second he could keep my parents locked up forever. Or worse.

The kind of control he had over them was unlike anything I had seen before. They moved like zombies, unable to control their own minds. His power was above and beyond anything I could even comprehend. And he was still after more.

And he wanted to make me *like him.*

I had to stop him. Somehow. I wasn't sure any amount of training could help me become strong enough to beat him head to head, and I couldn't drain him if he was beating the snot out of me. I rubbed my face on my forearms, trying to dry my tears, trying to soothe the tension headache that grew, trying to fight exhaustion, trying to think.

I just had to find the right time.

He had to have some weakness. And I would find out what it was.

The next day, I was woken by dawn's pink light streaming into where I lay on the tiled dining room floor. I blinked, looking around, hoping it was all just a dream, but the state of the room proved it had really happened. The place was trashed. Sticky bits of stir-fry congealed in blobs around the room, surrounded by spray patterns of rice. Family photos lay scattered, escaped from their smashed frames.

Terry was the leech. And he had my parents.

I picked up the closest photo, of Mom, Dad, and I, dressed up as baby owls for book week when I was seven. Looking at it almost tipped me into the abyss of hopeless despair.

But then, a cold resolve took control. And with it came a plan of action.

I didn't dare call Limbus. I sent them a text saying I had the flu and wouldn't be coming in for training. In case Terry was tracking my phone, I wanted proof I hadn't outed him. I figured that was the kind of power he'd have, in his position.

I tested my body, stiff and sore from sleeping on tiles and probably also from getting thrown almost clean through a wall. I shuffled to the closest window and looked out onto the street. A cop car was parked a few houses down, right on the corner.

It wasn't Terry, but if he was police captain now, he wouldn't even need to use his empath suggestion powers to have someone keeping an eye on me.

I checked a back window. There didn't seem to be anyone watching the footpath that ran along the back of our yard. Only from where the cop was parked on the corner, he'd be able to see both ends of where the path came back out again.

But I was placing my bets on Terry not knowing about Dean's bike.

I changed out of my food and tear-stained clothes, and into a pair of Mom's cargo pants and one of Dean's biggest hoodies. Along with the full-head helmet, I hoped that would be enough of a disguise to make me unrecognizable. I stuffed some granola bars in my pockets, and left my phone on the table.

I went into the garage and carried Dean's dirt bike up into the house, through the laundry door and out the back gate. I was a sweaty mess by the time I got there, but as I edged out onto the pathway I couldn't see anyone around.

My hands shook as I swung my leg over the bike. I was glad Dean had shown me once how to ride, but now I had to do it on my own it all seemed very scary.

The engine roared to life. Adrenalin and fear raced through my veins. The bike throbbed beneath me. "Here goes nothing."

I wobbled back and forth for a moment, bunny hopping and having to put my foot down a few times before plowing into a neighbor's fence. But I managed to straighten up as I left the path and went out onto the road.

I kept a slow and steady pace, checking the rear-vision mirror a few times, but the cop hadn't followed me. I was free.

And I was going to find Terry.

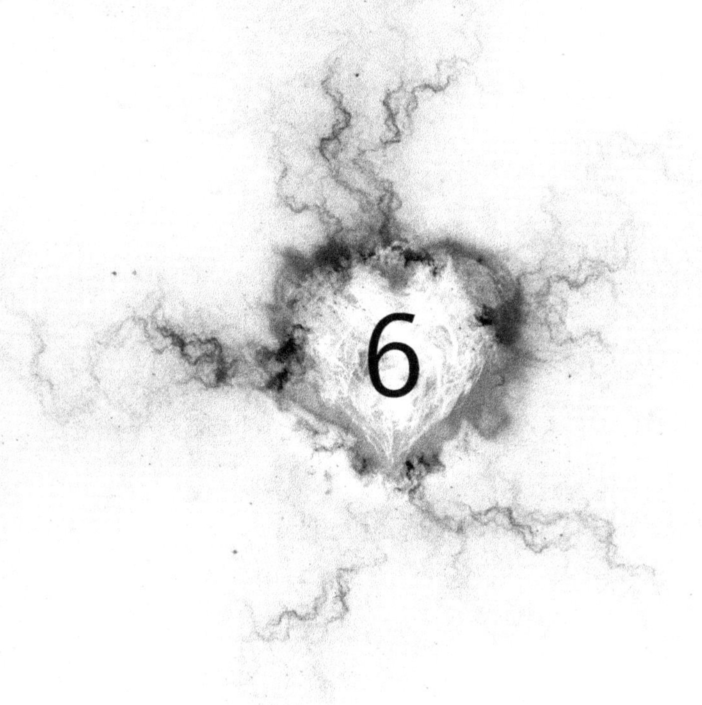

6

My first day of stalking Terry yielded nothing. He spent the entire time at the police station and stayed late. I tried to wait for him to head back to his house, or anywhere alone, but was too exhausted to keep my eyes open.

I went home, parking Dean's bike a block away and sneaking in through the neighbors' backyards. I crawled into bed, and even my tears and pains couldn't keep me awake.

The next day, I trailed Terry from function to function. First, a press announcement on Main Street. Then lunch at the golf club with the mayor. Then an inspiring speech for new cadets visiting the precinct. I kept my distance and kept my helmet on whenever I could, staying out of the way and out of sight.

Both nights, I went home exhausted and without having found any chance to take out Terry, or any clue as to how. Both days, I left my phone at home and went into full-on stalker mode. Obsession drove me. I barely ate, spoke to no one—there was only Terry.

Three days later, in the late evening, I was about to give up for the night when Terry came out of the station. He was talking to another officer. "I'm going to head home and have dinner with my family. They haven't seen me in a while. I bet you got this, right?"

I couldn't see the other officer's face, but he nodded and Terry smiled, patting him on the shoulder. I ducked back behind the alley wall as he walked over to his car and pulled out.

After giving him some distance, I followed on Dean's bike. I kept the lights off. The slight night-vision I got from my empath powers and abundant street lighting was enough to see by. I also kept my emotions as off as possible. I didn't want Terry to sense my raging hatred for him, so I locked it all away. I channeled Dean, trying to be cool, calm, and contained. I doubted I'd become a blocker overnight, but it was surprisingly easier than I thought to shut it all out when I didn't want to be feeling all that pain.

A few days had given me a lot of practice in reining in my emotions, and also at riding Dean's bike. I had been almost constantly on it during daylight hours.

We left the town and headed up a curvy mountain road, surrounded by pine forest. I leaned into the curves, the cold air whipping past me. I knew Terry lived on the outskirts of town, but I had never been there. I didn't think my parents had ever been there either. This was my chance to find out where he lived. Where he slept.

With fewer vehicles on the road, and less lighting, I slowed down and kept back, worried a few times I'd lost him. Then, up ahead I saw him slow down in front of a tall, ornate iron gate which opened automatically for him.

I stopped and waited as he drove down the long gravel drive and turned his lights off. I turned my own engine off and rolled the bike over behind a thick redwood.

I left the helmet behind too; there were enough bushes and shadows to keep hidden in, and I was worried the shiny surface would reflect light and be spotted. I crept up to the property on foot, and climbed over the high brick walls, checking for security cameras as I went.

As I came around through the side garden and saw the

house itself, my mouth dropped. It was a mansion—massive and richly detailed, like something out of a movie.

Through the lit windows I could easily see inside, where chandeliers shimmered, dangling from the ceilings in most rooms, gilt-framed paintings were hung on the walls, and everything looked pristine, stunning, and unjustifiably expensive. There was no way Terry afforded all of this on his cop salary alone, no matter how many promotions he had arranged for himself.

Jake and his team's lifestyle seemed a much more fitting explanation. So much for all of Terry's greater good talk. He was using his powers to serve himself.

I ducked behind a formally sculpted hedge. From there, I could see into a kitchen and dining room where people moved about. There was a tall, beautiful blonde woman wearing a neat fifties-style dress and apron, moving plates from the kitchen to the dinner table. There, two infant children with strawberry-blond hair sat in high chairs. The woman looked really nervous, fussing over the layout of dishes and center ornaments on the table. The kids weren't fussing, but their heads drooped. They looked wiped out. Should they have been up so late?

Terry walked in behind the woman and kissed her on the cheek. She froze for a moment, then spun around and took

Terry into her arms, kissing him and smiling broadly. He patted her on the butt, then rubbed each child on the head, waking them and making them look around, bleary-eyed, before taking his seat at the head of the table.

The little boy's chin wobbled, his mouth opened wide, and his face scrunched up.

The woman spotted his reaction to being disturbed and rushed over beside the child when the loud wail escaped his lips. She knocked a spoon out of a dish as she went, splattering soup across the table. She looked panicked, staring between the soup and the screaming child, the other kid now set off as well. And then to Terry who had risen from his seat and stalked towards her.

"Oh, enough!" Terry snapped, and the crying boy's face went blank, along with the girl beside him. "I come home from working all day and have to deal with this? Can't you keep the kids under control and serve a simple meal? Do I really ask so much from you?"

Terry's hand snapped out and he grabbed his wife by the throat. He picked her up in the air, holding her there for a long moment while she clawed at his hand, her eyes bulging.

I gasped loudly, putting my hand over my own mouth as fear and anger rushed through me.

Terry's body went rigid and he put his wife back onto her feet. His head whipped towards the window. I ducked down flat onto the ground.

Calm. Controlled. Cold. Feel nothing.

I counted to twenty. No doors opened, no footsteps came, and no one grabbed me from my hiding place.

"Clear this mess up," Terry commanded, and I dared to look up again.

His wife held her throat, her shoulders heaving with hard breaths, and tears streamed down her face. Terry patted her on the shoulder and just like that, she was smiling. She kissed him on the cheek, and fluttered around the room, cleaning and serving as he sat down again.

I backed away, keeping to the shadows until I got over the wall and then bolted for the bike.

That poor woman. Those kids … how long have they been his prisoners?

I couldn't help them yet, but I might be able to help my parents. If Terry was just sitting down to a large meal, it could be enough time to get back to the station and possibly break out my parents. It was a long shot, but if I could do it, I could take them to Limbus and then let everyone know what was happening.

I grabbed the helmet and bike and rolled it farther away before starting it up. I didn't think he could hear it all the way out there, but I didn't want anything tipping him off. I sped back to town, ditching the bike in the alleyway I'd been staking out the station from. If I were able to get my parents out, we'd need some other transportation. I would come back for it later.

I left the helmet on and visor down. It restricted my vision a bit, but I was pretty sure there would be surveillance cameras here. Sneaking around the outside of the police building, I crouched down behind a side door I'd seen a couple of police using for smoke breaks.

I extended my senses, feeling for the presence of nearby emotions. It wasn't quite X-ray vision, but enough to give me a feeling of where people where around me.

Like when my parents had waited angrily outside of Dean's door when I had been in there with him without permission. I missed them all so much already. The idea of sneaking into the station terrified me, but I had to get my parents back, and then I could get Dean back.

I kept low and hid in the shadow of a dumpster until I sensed someone on the other side of the door. Just one person, by the feel of it. The handle turned. I was right. One female officer pushed out through the door and wandered over near a streetlight, cigarette in hand. I dashed to the door before it swung closed and slipped inside.

I had been in the station only once before. I must have been eight or nine, and Terry had taken my class on a tour. Always smiling. Always helping out. Had he leeched anyone then? *Had he even known he was an empath at that time?*

I roughly remembered where the holding cells were, and sprinted down the hallway on soft feet, as silent as I could.

I sensed two people headed my way and I backed up behind a filing cabinet. They went the other way at the corner of the corridor. They were eerily calm and content in their work, despite the late hour. It gave me little power to work with, and I wondered how much of that was their captain's doing.

Up around the corner, I snuck through an unoccupied bullpen office that backed onto the holding cells. I peeked out from behind a cluttered desk. *Mom, Dad.* They were there. I could have shouted for joy. But two guards stood in front of the cell, their expressions stiff and determined. Under orders, I was sure.

I knelt down and ground my teeth. I had to do something, but there wasn't enough emotion at the moment to build up my strength and speed. It was the happiest, calmest police station ever.

My eyes fell on the fire alarm on the wall beside me. This might be my only chance. I could only risk hiding under a desk for so long, and had no other way to get the guards out of there. I shrugged. It was worth a shot. I waited until the guards looked away, then lunged up, pulled the alarm, then dove back under the desk.

A high, jangling bell rang throughout the station. I stayed completely under cover.

"We have a drill scheduled?" one of the guards asked.

"Captain Pence said we should keep an eye out for anything that seemed off," the other replied. "Let's go and see what's going on."

They walked right past where I was crouched. I held my breath.

As soon as they were through the door, I grabbed a ring of keys from a rack on the wall and hurried to my parents' cell. Everything was labelled so it didn't take me long to get the door unlocked. I swung it wide open.

"Quick, let's go!" I hissed.

They both looked up at me, confused.

"It's me, Livvy." I popped the visor up, even though they should have known my voice. I frowned.

"Lollipop, so nice to see you." Dad beamed, but he didn't

move from his seat.

Chills prickled up my spine. "We have to go, like, *now.*"

"Why?" Mom laughed softly. "We're perfectly happy here. We're happy to stay here as long as we have to. We're not going anywhere."

No, no, no. I squatted down in front of them, grabbing their hands. "You have to snap out of this. Terry is controlling you. You don't want to be here."

They just smiled, shrugged, and didn't move.

I had never compelled anyone with my powers before, but I tried then. I focused all my willpower on making them listen to me, making them think that my suggestion was exactly what they wanted to do, *had* to do. "Come with me, please," I pleaded.

Neither of them even blinked. Terry's powers were just too strong, even without him being there. I knew Jake's powers had some hangover time before they wore off, and he had just one proesthian's worth of power.

I growled in frustration. There had to be another way. I considered trying to carry them but wasn't strong enough. Maybe if I still had four empaths' worth of power in me I could have, but not anymore.

The alarm blaring overhead cut out suddenly.
Silence.

The cops knew there was no fire. They'd be back any second.

I gripped my parents' hands and pulled them up to kiss them. "I'll come back for you, I promise." Then I flicked my visor back down and turned away.

I quickly locked the cell again and put the keys back, hoping I could get out unnoticed except for the unexplained false alarm. But as I passed by the desk I'd hid under, something caught my eye. A kraft brown folder lay there, with a label on the front that read, "Limbus."

That is so very, very far from good.

I could sense people just down the hall, but paused to flip the folder open. I gasped. There were pictures of Dr. and Mr. Crossman inside. A picture of the pink-haired agent. One of Rayni, the day she and Ash picked me up from school.

And it was all there, on a detective's desk. My heart raced. Was Terry getting his station to investigate Limbus for him? To hunt empaths for him?

What could be worse that this?

"Hey, you! Don't move!"

Two cops stood in the doorway, their guns aimed at me.

Oh, yeah.

That could be worse.

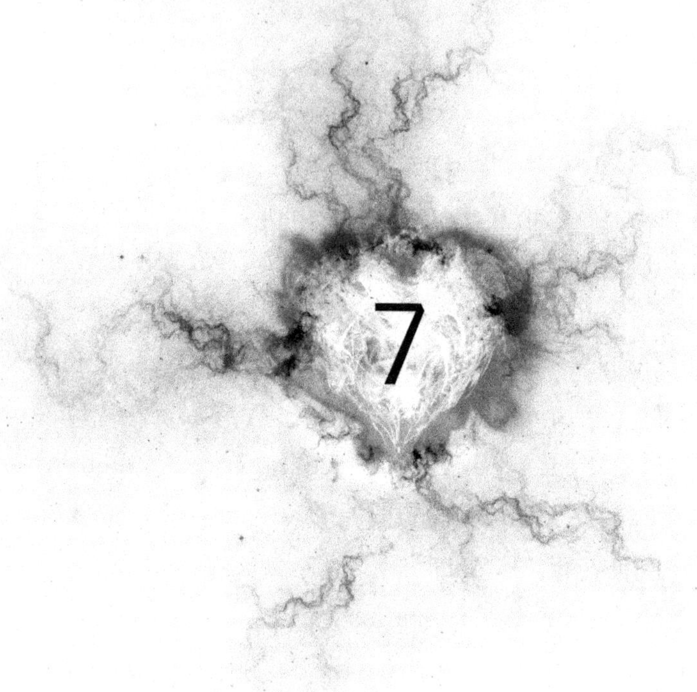

7

couldn't talk my way out of this one. Not that it was a particular talent I possessed, but I didn't want the cops to have more reason to work out who I was and pass that info on to Terry.

I threw the folder in my hands at the men. It broke apart in mid-air, paper exploding everywhere. A rush of fear and anger spilled from them to me. It was just what I needed.

I absorbed those emotions and focused my powers. Before the fluttering sheets had reached the floor, I raced toward the cops.

As I reached them, I dropped and slid along the floor on my knees. I grabbed one each of their ankles, and with a sharp tug, toppled them over onto their faces.

I launched back to my feet and dashed out the door without looking back. I hoped I hadn't hurt them much. I didn't want to hurt any of them. But I had to get out of there.

I took off at top speed down the hallway, no longer worried about being spotted, just trying to get out as fast as I could. Three more police rounded the hallway corner in front of me. The view of my blurringly fast figure drove fear through them and into me, sending me faster. I kicked off the wall beside me, ricocheted off the opposite wall, and flipped myself over through the gap between the cops and the ceiling, spinning my body with sheer speed and instinct. I hit the floor on the other side on my knees, rolled forward in a somersault, then sprang up onto my feet again. I reached the side exit before they'd even had a chance to turn around.

I burst out of the station and into the cold night air. A gust of visible breath fogged the inside of my helmet as I panted hard.

But I didn't dare stop.

I fled to the alley and took off on Dean's bike, adrenaline drilling through my whole body.

I'd made it out. I could have almost screamed with relief.

But I knew it was bound to be short-lived. A helmeted intruder was going to be something reported to the station captain. And security videos would be reviewed. And it would be clear to Terry just from context, even without seeing my face, who I was. I shuddered to think what he was going to do once he found out.

Because I hadn't been able to save my parents.

Terry had my whole life in his hands.

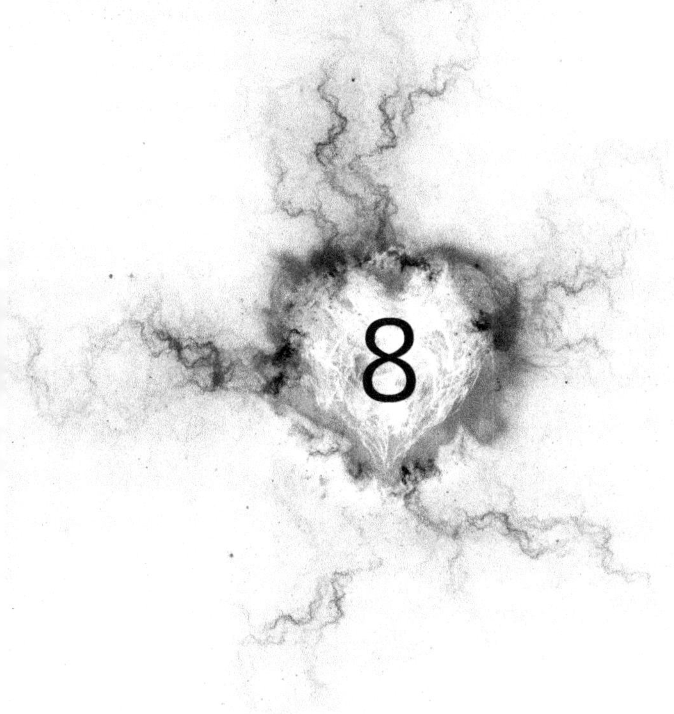

8

I sat slumped on the couch, staring at the blank television screen.

After getting home from the police station, I had fallen asleep there, and when I'd woken in the morning, I couldn't find the energy to go out again. There seemed to be no reason to keep hunting Terry. It all felt so pointless. I was sure he was going to come to me any second now, to punish me for trying to free my parents.

So I just sat, and stared, and waited.

My stomach grumbled. There wasn't a lot left in the fridge or pantry that I knew how to make into a meal. Empty pizza boxes were already piled up on the coffee table alongside a handful of unopened letters.

The last cash I'd rustled up from around the house had been spent on fuel for the bike. I hadn't wanted to use my parents' credit cards for anything other than fast food deliveries, worried if I used them out of the house I'd be tracked. Until last night, I'd hoped I'd gotten away with the illusion I hadn't stepped foot outside.

There were some missed calls from Limbus, but I sent them another text from my mom's phone, explaining I was still sick. Last time they activated my tracker, it flashed, so I figured they bought my excuse and hadn't felt the need to check in on me yet.

If only I could go there. I wanted more than anything to zoom down to Limbus on Dean's bike, and then climb into the hospital bed beside him and curl up, holding him. I hadn't seen him since Terry took my parents and I felt his absence like a hole in the chest.

But going to Limbus was too big of a risk. Terry was already investigating them. He knew of their existence, but I hadn't seen any photos of the Bellston Main Limbus building in the folder. I could only hope he never found out where they were. And that meant keeping my distance, from them, and from Dean.

I whimpered and flopped over onto my side, crushing a crinkly, empty chip packet.

A knock on the door reverberated through the empty house.

I was on shaky feet in a flash, desperate to bolt. *He's come for me.*

But … why is he knocking?

I tiptoed hesitantly toward the front door. I extended my senses, trying to pull in any emotion from the other side. *Regret. Fear. Sadness.* No way it was Terry. Curious, I cracked the door open.

Standing on the other side was Dean's father. He looked worse off than he did the last time that I'd seen him. His gray eyes twitched over red cheeks, and his nose ran. There were holes in his shirt and sweatpants, and he only wore flip-flops. The sky above him was gray and heavy, and a cool breeze made me shiver.

"Mr. Lasslow?" I squeaked through the gap.

He wobbled, obviously drunk. But the anger he'd shown in the past wasn't there. "I want to talk to my son." He squinted at me. "Tell Dean I want to talk to him."

Oh. Oh, no. What was I supposed to tell him? The truth? His son was an empath and was drained of all his powers, and was lying in a coma in a secret agency headquarters? That was enough to confuse a sober person, much less a drunk one. I sighed and stepped out on the porch, shutting the door quickly behind me before he could decide to push past and go searching for his son.

"How did you find us?"

He held up a piece of paper with my mother's handwriting on it. "They sent me a letter. Gave me your address. In case of emergencies, it says."

Emergencies. My whole life was currently an emergency, and this man, who'd insulted me to my face more than once, showed up drunk? Wanting something?

I scowled. "Is this an emergency? Because Dean's not here and even if he was, I doubt he'd want to talk to you."

"He's my son. He'll talk to me if I say he has to talk to me." He spat the words, but shuffled uncomfortably back and forth.

"He doesn't belong to you. He's not a thing to be controlled, like you tried to control your wife." I stepped closer, uncontrollable anger burned through me, tightening my fists. "You wouldn't let her go, wouldn't deal with your own emotions from losing her, and wouldn't help Dean deal with his. He was a child who needed to mourn his mom's death, but you left him feeling like it wasn't even okay for him to cry. He had to crush all of his emotions so completely it broke him." *And he became a blocker. And he was drained because of it, just when he was starting to heal, just when he was starting to open up* … I thrusted both palms into Mr. Lasslow's chest and knocked him off his feet, down onto the front path. "You broke *everything*."

He looked up at me from the ground, his eyes wide and watering. The look of complete heartache on his face made my stomach turn.

It wasn't him I was angry at. Not really. I hadn't wanted to hurt him, but I couldn't deal with him here, now, on top of everything else. I just wanted him gone.

I rubbed my eyes, finding them wet as well. "Just get out of here. Get sober. Deal with your emotions instead of drinking them away, and maybe you'll be in a place for once where you could help Dean deal with his. I know you lost your wife, but Dean lost her *and* you. He needs his father back. He needs you to be able to look him in the eye and tell him you're sorry for the way you left him all alone in the world."

He stumbled back up to his feet and looked around wildly, his teeth clenched. For a second, I thought he was going to rush me. But then he wiped his eyes with the back of his sleeve, spat into the herb garden, and hobbled away crookedly, swearing and muttering.

I felt about the same as I shuffled back into the lonely house.

I was way harsher than I'd needed to be, venting all my anger out onto Mr. Lasslow, but I really did want him to be better. For Dean.

If Dean ever woke up again.

My eyes filled with hot tears.

I wish Dean was here. I wish anyone was here.

On the hall table in front of me, my phone flashed and hummed. I stared at it for a moment, fearful of what could be on the other end. Slowly, I reached for it, blinking my eyes clear so I could read the screen.

A call from Nati. I sobbed in relief, and need. I needed to hear her voice. I needed to not be alone anymore.

I answered, trying to hide my shaking breath. "Hey, Nati."

"Hey girl," she said, and I could hear the smile in her tone. "So, I was thinking, since you like to play hooky from school these days, you wanna come over and do a little sisterly bonding?"

I bit my lip. I wanted to see her so badly, but could I, without putting her in danger?

Nati took my silence as an answer. "I know you're probably stuck like glue to Dean, but I haven't seen you in forevs. I need you over here, no buts, buttface. As long as you aren't contagious."

I looked around my empty home. I had to get out of there before I snapped entirely. I'd just have to sneak there the best

I could, but with all the secret coming and going I'd been doing, I'd learned a few new routes that I hoped might still be unnoticed. "Screw it. Yeah. I'll be over as soon as it's dark."

"Holy herringbones, the sky is going to fall!" She giggled. "I'll meet you out back of my house so you can get in the gate."

"Wait." I was terrified I'd made the wrong decision, that this was going to be another mistake, another loss. For all I knew, Terry was bugging my calls. But he must already know Nati was my friend. If he'd wanted more hostages, he'd had plenty of chances. Still … "Instead, can we meet"—I bit my tongue, careful not to say too much—"at that place with the crazy sundaes?"

I held my breath, hoping she wouldn't give it away.

"Brilliant idea! Ice-cream for dinner it is!"

"Perfect," I replied. "See you soon."

I hung up, smiling, my heart pounding. Even if Terry knew I was going out, as long as I didn't get followed, he wouldn't know where.

It was only early afternoon, so I waited, pacing anxiously around the house, talking myself out of cancelling. Soon, the sky through the windows darkened, and the heavy clouds released a sprinkle of rain across the suburb.

I grabbed a large black raincoat of Dad's, put it on over

Dean's hoodie, and left my phone behind. Peeking out a front window, I saw the cop car still sitting at the corner up the street, right in view of the front of the house and the exits to the back pathway.

I crept out into the backyard, and listened, extending my senses to check for anyone outside. The rain had everyone indoors, and created a gray veil over the world, almost inviting me to disappear into it.

I jumped over the neighbor's fence and dashed across their yard. I went like that all the way to the end of the block, over and across every neighbors' property, over the pathway itself, and continued on until I reached the yard at the opposite corner of the block to the cop. Rain splattered my face, and my fingers were chilled as I watched through the palings for my opportunity.

A few cars passed by, driving slowly, lights and wipers on. Then, a few minutes later, there was a removals truck. I pulled the hood drawstrings tight, zipped out through the gate, and grabbed the back of the truck, jumping onto the bumper.

I travelled like that for two blocks until I hoped I was clear, and before anyone saw me riding that way, then hopped back off and went to collect Dean's bike.

I reached the games arcade dripping wet, my fingers numb

and my cheeks burning.

Leaving my hood up, I carried my helmet, my raincoat rolled up under one arm, and walked through the dinging games and hyped-up children to the secluded booths up the back. Screens flashed around me of colorful characters racing cute cars, kawaii photo booths, and gritty shoot-'em-ups. One kid was being way too zealous with the Whac-A-Mole. I hoped Terry wouldn't find us there, since I'd only mentioned food, and this wasn't strictly a café or diner.

I spotted Nati in one of the booths, happily scrolling through her phone, ringlets hanging down over a sequin-streaked shirt.

"Why do you look like you just escaped a super-max through the sewage drain?" she asked as I ducked down onto the seat across from her.

I wiped matted wet hair off my face, readjusted my hood, and faked a laugh. "Thought I'd walk over."

"You are so weird." She frowned, and I could *feel* her worry. She eyed me up and down, then held my gaze until I had to look away or risk bursting into tears.

She tsked. "All right. What's going on? And don't BS me. I know something is up. The look on your face is breaking my heart."

I gaped. Gulped. Crumpled. I wanted to brush it off, make

up some excuse, but I had nothing left in me. I hadn't told her before because I didn't want her to think I was crazy, because it was all so much. But now, it had all become so much I would go crazy if I *didn't* tell her. I stared at her with tears in my eyes and just exploded.

I spilled everything. From the first time I met Jake, to Dean's powers, to where he was now and how the leech stole my parents. The only detail I left out was who the leech was.

Her mouth hung open and she just watched and listened until I finally stopped rambling.

She sat back in her chair and crossed her arms. "I ... wow, that's some crazy stuff. Hold on, let me process." She waved a waiter over and ordered two of the most extreme ice-cream-piled-on-sugar-piled-on-candy sundaes they offered. "That's to help us process," she told me, and then leaned forward on the table toward me. "Okay. Superpowers. Crazy adventures. I mean, it makes sense. It makes total sense, actually."

"Uh, really?" I wiped my eyes with the sides of the hood.

"Uh, really." She echoed me sarcastically. "Weeks away from school all the time? Surviving roof cave-ins? Getting abducted by shifty clandestine agents? I kind of already figured things weren't in the realm of normality for you anymore."

I pouted bashfully. "Sorry I didn't tell you sooner."

"Nah, I get that this is an area requiring total secrecy." She hushed up quickly as the waiter brought our sundaes over, pausing until he was gone. "You're in some seriously dangerous doo-doo right now. And I have no ideas for anything I can do to help."

I picked some cotton candy off the ice-cream and let it melt on my tongue. "This is helping already. I just needed to get it out. Dealing with all this, all alone—it was eating me away, rotting me from the inside."

Nati wrinkled her nose and reached out, taking my hand. "You need a place to stay? Can you come to my house?"

I shook my head. "Not safe for you or your family."

Nati sighed and stabbed her spoon at her ice-cream. We devoured our sundaes in silence for a while. "Babe, this sucks. I really wish I could do something. Can't you blast me with energy and give me powers, too?"

I snickered, and then sniffled. "I wish. I wish you could be in this with me, but I'm also happy that you're not. It's hard, being like this, having these powers when they still aren't enough to save the people you love."

Nati slid off her seat, came over to my side of the booth, and wrapped her arms around me. "You're enough. I know you've got this, Livvy. You know why?"

"Why?"

"Because even before this whole superpower deal, you were a hero. I would always see you, how no matter what came your way, you would tackle it head-on, with heart and guts. You're the best person I know."

"I don't feel like I've been very heroic lately," I muttered. *Dean's dad probably doesn't think I am, either.*

She just shrugged. "You're in a bad place, and I mean, come on, kind of understandable. But you're going to pick yourself up. You'll look inside yourself and see you have what you need to win this. You have enough love inside you to change people, change the world. If you have emotion-based superpowers, you have a heart that is unstoppable."

My nose wrinkled and I hugged Nati back. Her words were exactly what I needed to hear. I had spent too long dwelling in places of fear and anger. I wanted to find my answer, my hope, my courage, in *love*. Because it was the one thing I was sure I had that Terry didn't.

"Thank you," I whispered. "I love you."

"I love you too." Nati placed a sugar-sticky kiss on my cheek. "Now, let's get seconds, 'kay?"

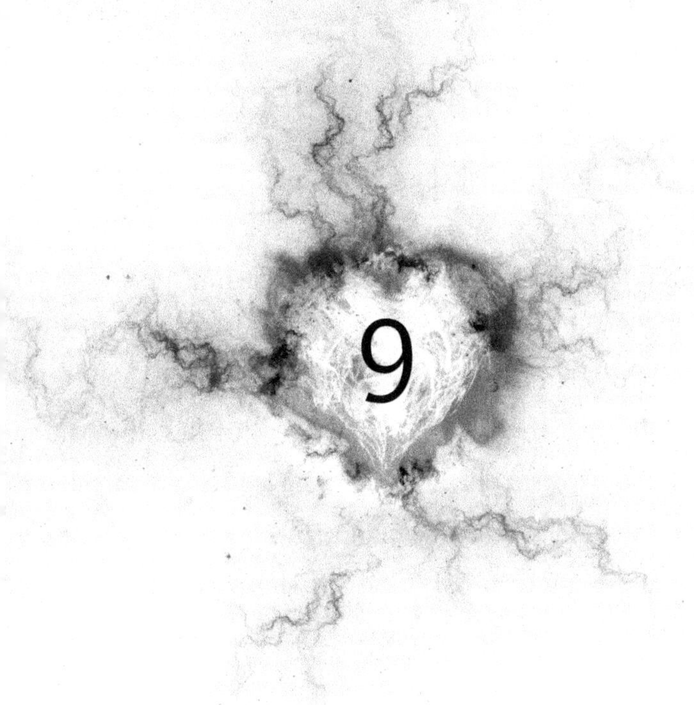

9

Bringing Dean's bike to a stop behind a parked SUV, I put one foot down against the curb so I could lean out far enough to see. Terry had pulled his cruiser over up ahead.

After the talk with Nati, my spirits had improved, and my determination grew with them. I'd started following Terry again, since he hadn't decided to come after me yet. Maybe he hadn't found out about what happened at the station, or hadn't worked out it was me, or perhaps he was just too arrogant to care. Regardless, I decided to continue my surveillance of him, to find a time to make my plan happen.

I would wait until he was alone.

I would take the first chance I could to drain him, before he suspects, before he can fight back

I would absorb everyone he held inside him.

And I would hope my heart was big enough to contain it all.

Nati believed I could do it. I just hoped she was right.

I'd followed Terry all the way down to Bellston Main, growing more worried all the way that he'd discovered Limbus's HQ. But we ended up on a small nightlife street with a club on the corner, an open-all-hours kebab store, a diner, and a Japanese restaurant.

Terry strolled into the diner, and through the window I watched him order at the counter, watched him flirt with the lady who served him his takeaway coffee. Watched how he didn't even pay.

When he came back out, he set his cup on the roof of the car while he checked his phone. Everything inside me wanted to take him down right then and there. But despite Nati's pep talk, I knew I had to be patient and at least wait until I wasn't in the middle of a busy street where everyone could watch me straight up assault a uniformed police captain.

He opened his car door and I started the bike again to continue the trail.

Then something in my chest thumped.

I put my hand to my heart and swallowed hard. Someone's emotions were raging nearby, and it was sinking right into me. Feelings of happiness, excitement, nervousness, and … *love*. And the emotions felt so familiar.

It was how I felt for Dean, the excitement and surprise of finding a love beyond anything I could have imagined.

As the sensation grew stronger, I realized that the familiarity wasn't just because I knew those feelings—it was because I recognized *the people* they came from.

My eyes darted, trying to find the source. A couple came out of the door to the Japanese restaurant, giggling and holding each other tightly. Both were tall, and both had hoods pulled up over their heads. The girl reached forward, her sleeve inching up. On her wrist was an orange Limbus tracking bracelet, and I glimpsed red hair.

Emma? What was she doing out here? And who was she with?

They turned, both looking up, and the light hit their faces.

Bastian? My jaw dropped. Emma and Bastian … *together?*

"What bizarro world is this?" I growled to myself.

Then it hit me. If I could feel them, so could the leech. And Terry knew about my adventures with Jake and Emma. He could have files. He could know what she looked like.

My eyes snapped back to the cop car. The coffee still sat

on top, but Terry wasn't there.

Where did you go? Panic brewed in my belly. "Get out of here," I begged in a whisper, watching Bastian and Emma strolling together into the tree-filled park down the street. They had no idea of the danger they were in, but I felt every part of it.

My eyes landed on Terry again, prowling out from behind a building, going toward the park entrance. His smile was dark and ominous. He'd sensed them. *He was hunting Emma.*

Once in the shadow of the trees, Terry picked up his pace. I had to do something, and I had to do it fast. My grip tightened on the handles of the bike.

I hit the gas and took off, speeding out onto the street. I skidded around the corner, and gunned it, jumping up the curb. People tumbled out of my way, yelling in my wake. I kept going. Racing across the grass of the park, I dodged trees and newly planted flower beds.

Bastian and Emma were right up ahead. Terry stalked behind them.

The happy emotions I'd been feeling from the couple shifted suddenly to fear, and Emma buckled, folding in the middle. Bastian caught her, oblivious to the cause standing just down the path from them, already draining Emma's life away.

Busy sapping Emma's powers, Terry also seemed oblivious to the roar of the bike racing toward him. I put my head down, aiming directly for him. I went faster, as fast as I could go.

At the last second, Terry looked up with wide eyes. I leaped from the bike, and it plowed into him. They tangled together, bouncing and dragging across the grass twenty feet in a roar of scraping metal.

I rolled across the ground and slid to a stop between Terry and Emma.

Pulling off my helmet, I looked back at her and Bastian.

Bastian shifted his focus between all of us, eyes squinting then going wide, his whole body shivering. He grabbed Emma's hand and started pulling her away. *He got it.* Elucidist powers were really something.

Emma held her ground though, staring at me like I was mad. "Livvy? What have you done to that cop?"

The bike lay on top of Terry and both were still, surrounded by a cloud of settling dust. I held my breath. I only wanted to stop him, not kill him. If he was dead, then Dean …

A low, angry groan came from beneath the bent metal.

I yelled, "He's the leech! You've got to go!"

Both of Emma's hands went to her mouth, her head shaking. "We can help—"

"We can't." Bastian's tone was crushed, yet determined. "I'm sorry Livvy. I'm so sorry."

I inhaled sharply, fear twisting its tendrils into my heart with his words. Bastian tugged harder at Emma's hand, and she looked at me one more time. "But—"

"Emma, we can't survive this. Livvy …" Bastian looked at me with sad eyes. "Livvy *can.*"

Emma's face crumpled, then she turned away and they ran. I watched as they took off, Emma using her proesthian speed to help Bastian move faster, and they disappeared into the shadows of the park. I nodded to myself. It was better they wouldn't be here for this, for what I had to do.

My body ached from hitting the ground. I pulled myself to my feet, holding tightly to my knees to keep upright. I dropped the helmet and took in a long, deep breath, pulling my powers into focus. Strength filled me and I stalked toward Terry, letting loose my pain and despair. *Losing Ash. Losing Marigold. Losing Dean. Losing my parents.* I let my grief swallow me so I could use it to swallow him.

I stood above Terry, who grumbled and twitched under the broken bike.

Darkness overwhelmed me, ravenous, angry, and cold, and I let it feed on Terry. I sensed the first touch of our consciousnesses.

Terry roared in anger, throwing the bike up and off of him. It flew through the air and crashed into a tree trunk behind me.

I gritted my teeth, tried to hold my focus. The drain on him wavered, failed. I couldn't get a grip on him; all the energy was too jumbled, too tightly packed, too massive. My own mind felt like it slipped and slid around in my body, and sometimes out of it.

Terry got to his feet, cricked his neck, and dusted off the front of his uniform. "What on earth do you think you're doing? You stupid girl."

"Stopping you!" I cried, pushing deeper into my despair, pushing the energy out toward him.

It seemed to have no effect at all.

He strolled toward me. I kicked him as hard as I could in the stomach. He braced, then kept coming. I swung wide, meeting his jaw with my fist. Blood splattered from his lips, but he kept coming. He grinned wide, blood covering his teeth, then backhanded me across the face so hard I flew through the air into the same tree the bike had hit.

My back cracked as it hit the trunk, and I tumbled down in an avalanche of broken bark, landing badly on the hot, pointed metal of the bike. I cried out, whimpered, and hurried to get back up.

Terry appeared in a flash by my side. His hand wrapped around my throat. My eyes went wide and I wheezed for air. I clawed onto his wrist as he lifted me up off my feet. Tears poured down my face. I swung my arms, my legs, but I couldn't reach him.

He's going to drain me. This is it.

I winced, waited. His grip tightened, crushing my throat, then he slammed me to the ground with bone-cracking force.

Air rushed from my lungs and I didn't have enough left to cry out.

Through pain-blurred eyes, I watched as Terry stood over me, shaking his head.

"I've known you since you were a little girl," he barked. "I've given you every opportunity, but you keep trying to fight me. Why? Trying to save your parents? Trying to drain me? Can't you see it's pointless? *I am a god.*"

He lifted one knee and brought his foot crashing down onto my ribs. I screamed, a dry, cracked scream, and curled into a ball.

"You could be too. That's what I'm trying to offer you. Be my apprentice, my disciple. I know you have it in you."

His foot landed again, deep in my lower back. Pain blinded me. Bile rose in my throat, hot and stinging. I tried to pull my body together, pull my powers into focus, but everything swirled.

"I'm offering you power. We could rule this world. If you'd stop being so stubborn."

Again and again he struck out, hard leather boots crushing me to a pulp.

"You've been brainwashed to think there are heroes and villains, good and evil, but real life isn't a fairy tale. One day, you'll understand that. Only power matters. And imagine how powerful we could be together."

He bent down over me, grabbing me by the top of the head, wrenching my face up close to his by my hair.

I lost all control of my emotions. I wept hard, useless tears for my own pain, for my imprisoned parents, for the love I shared with Dean that felt so impossibly lost. I roared in anger and fear, my throat as raw as my bloodied, bruised body, as raw as my heart. I tried to lift an arm to fight back, but it wobbled weirdly. I whimpered.

I have to survive this. I have to win this.

Bastian said I could survive this.

"Next time, I won't stop," Terry hissed into my face. "This is your last chance to consider my offer. Join me, or you will become just another vessel to drain the power from. Either way, you will only make me stronger."

He slammed the back of my head into the ground. My eyes

went wide and then fought to close. The entire world spun around me, falling, falling into darkness. *Bastian said I could survive. Bastian ... said ...*

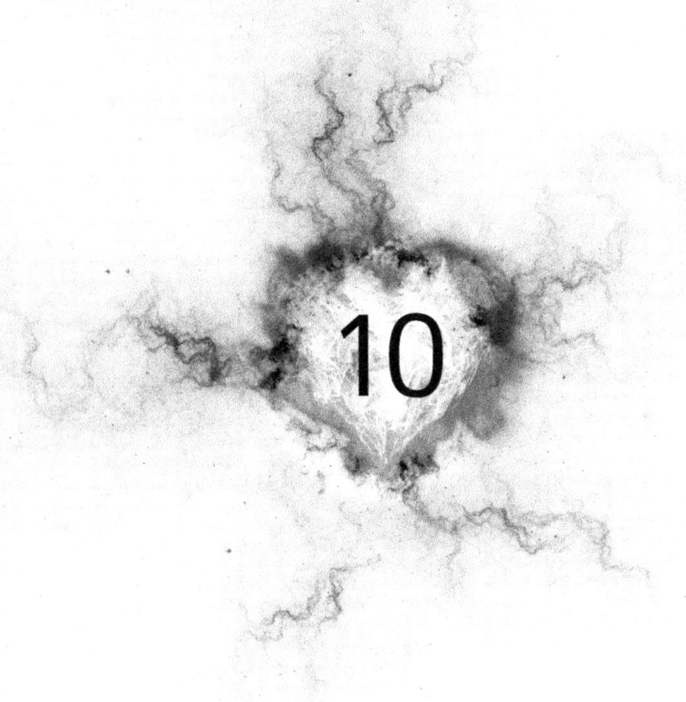

10

Reality flashed around me in painful, disjointed moments. In between was only fog and darkness.

Two blurry figures, argued. My hands moved, held and controlled by someone else. I thought I was crying.

I was alone. I could feel every sharp twig and pebble pressing up from the cold ground into my mangled body. Everything was pain. Light flashed. Barely enough strength remained to remember to breathe.

Then darkness. Then more voices. Surrounding, urgent. I screamed when I was lifted and moved. Agony smashed my consciousness out of existence.

I came back to a strange sensation of softness rattling beneath me. I was moving, rolling. There was so much light, glaring down in bursts overhead right through my aching, puffy eyelids. I tried to reach my hands up to block it but someone grabbed them and put them back down by my side.

"Livvy?" It sounded like Dr. Crossman. I couldn't see, my face swollen up around my eyes. "Don't try and talk. Just stay still. We've got you."

"Get her over on the table," Felix yelled out somewhere above my head.

I was lifted, slid effortlessly to the side by unseen hands. Something sharp entered the back of my hand. The pain began to fade, and I faded with it.

I slipped into a deep sleep, floating through a darkened dream world. I could feel the coolness of Dean nearby, shifting to warmth, like he was wrapping his arms over my shoulders and holding me close. I could smell the ylang-ylang fragrance of my mom's candle collection, and hear the laughter of my father in the distance. I could taste the sugar-sweet friendship of Nati. I couldn't move, and everything remained dark. But I wasn't afraid. I wanted to stay there, safe from pain, safe from suffering. Safe in the darkness.

But the world around me began to shudder and shake. All

of my emotions surged forward, slamming hard into my chest. I could hear Terry's loud maniacal laughter all around me and panic crept through my veins.

I screamed out. "No! I won't be like you! You can't have me!"

There was a gentle pressure on my shoulder. My heart rate slowed, and a calm warmth spread through me. I could hear Rayni's voice near my ear. "Livvy, it's just a dream. You're safe. Just open your eyes and you'll see. You're safe."

I nodded in understanding, my brain quickly switching from dream mode to awake, helped by Rayni's control over my emotions. I took a deep breath, slowly opening my crusted-shut eyes.

I was in the ward at Limbus. Rayni stood beside me, and behind her, sitting in a row on the side of an empty bed, were Sway, Emma, and Bastian. *They're okay. They got away.* I swallowed relief down my dry throat.

Dr. Crossman placed a straw to my lips. I sipped the iced water slowly, gratefully. Felix checked my IV lines and blood pressure.

"How are you feeling?" Dr. Crossman asked. "We've got you on some pretty strong pain relief but let us know if it's not enough."

I looked down at my body in the bed. My left forearm was in a cast. My mouth tasted bloody. I could feel a low-level ache in my back and head, but didn't want it all gone. I didn't want to be numb completely. I had survived. I was alive, and the pain reminded me of that. "I'm okay. I'm fine."

"Kids these days have a strange definition of fine," Felix muttered. Then he patted me on the knee and I tried not to wince. "Your proesthian powers give you slightly faster healing though so you should really be fine soon, but I suggest staying in bed for now in case of complications."

Mr. Crossman folded his arms over his chest. "We are really glad you're okay, Olivia. But what in the world were you doing out there? We thought you were home with your parents, sick, then we found you like this in the park after you pressed your emergency button."

"I don't remember doing that," I mumbled, my head still foggy.

"Unsurprising. You've been out for fifteen hours." Dr. Crossman checked the watch on her tracker. "It looked like you'd driven a motorbike into a tree. But this clearly wasn't just a bike accident. What happened?"

I licked my lips and frowned. I wondered if I could pretend I didn't remember anything. I slowly turned my head. It crushed me to see all the others Terry had drained there beside me. I had done everything I could and failed. I didn't know what else to do.

Mr. Crossman put his hands on his hips. "We've been trying

to reach your parents, but no one's answering the phone or the front door. Olivia, you have to tell us what's going on."

My lips wrinkled with sadness, making my words shaky. "The leech did this."

Dr. Crossman's eyebrows went up. "Are you sure it was him? This isn't his normal behavior. I mean, he's certain to be in an unhinged and violent state of mind, but you weren't drained."

"I'm sure. I know who he is. I've been following him for a while."

Rayni gasped beside me, and I shied away from her confusion and disappointment.

"Who is it?" Mr. Crossman demanded.

I shook my head. "I can't tell you."

"What? Why not?" Dr. Crossman's professionalism cracked and she cried, "Why do you feel like you have to do everything alone? Why don't you trust us?"

"I do trust you. I wish I could have come to you. But he has my parents!"

Dr. Crossman put a hand over her mouth. "Oh, Olivia." She came over and sat on the side of my bed. "How long? Since you first called in sick? You should have told us. We could have helped."

"You don't understand what he's like, how strong he is. If I say any more, if anyone goes after him, my parents stand no chance."

Mr. Crossman seemed confused still. "Why? Why has he taken your parents? What does he want from you?"

He's a friend of the family. I've known him since I was eight. "He knows what I did, draining Jake and the others. He thinks I'm like him. He's power crazy, wants me to join him." I lifted my bandaged arm. "This was my last invitation."

Dr. Crossman stood back up and paced. "This is madness. You have to tell us who he is. We have to stop him."

"He's *unstoppable*. I started following him after he took my parents, hoping for some chance. Last night, when I saw …"

Bastian and Emma both had scared looks on their faces, and Bastian gave a tiny shake of his head. At first, I thought they just didn't want their forbidden date to be discovered, but then I realized they were actually helping me out. Because they knew who the leech was too. They'd seen him. They were keeping the secret too, for me.

"I thought I saw him go to attack someone, so I ran my bike into him. I tried. I tried to drain him and get everyone back, but he's too strong." My words devolved into sobs.

Rayni took my hand, all her calming ability lost in our

shared grief.

Mr. Crossman, Dr. Crossman, and Felix all stared at each other for a long moment. "We need to contact the agency heads." Dr. Crossman's voice had grown cold. "If he's really that powerful, has become this bold and violent, it may not be worth trying to capture him anymore. We may just need to take him out. Otherwise, who knows how many people he could hurt?"

"What? No," I said, pulling myself up in bed. "What about Dean? And the others? If the leech dies, they're gone for good."

"Then you have to tell us who he is so we have a chance of catching him before he gets any stronger, or hurts more people," Mr. Crossman replied.

"But then the people he'll hurt are my parents." My teeth ground together in frustration. "It's like I have to choose between my parents and Dean. This isn't fair. I can't tell you who he is and I won't let you kill him."

The machines I was hooked up to whirred and beeped wildly. Felix's one larger eye grew even bigger. "Whoa. Time out. Shh, shh, happy thoughts time," he sang to me, then gave the Crossmans a firm look.

Dr. Crossman sighed deeply and crossed her arms. "All right, enough for now. But Olivia, I want you to really think about the consequences here. We cannot afford to have civilian casualties in this."

"But we can afford to have empath ones?" I snapped back.

Her expression softened. "In this situation, we may not have a choice. These things aren't easy decisions. This room is filled with our friends and loved ones too."

I turned my head away. A few beds down, there was Dean. And Ash. Mr. Kairu with his faithful cat, Kimmy, on the end of his bed. Old Mr. Holbrook from the institute, and three more grown-ups I never knew, but the Crossmans had.

"Time for the patient to rest," Felix ordered.

Dr. Crossman patted the bed beside me, and she and her husband walked away, whispering together. Rayni, Sway, and Felix followed. Emma hopped up, and for a moment, she grabbed my fingers and squeezed them. Her lips were pressed thin, then she and Bastian left too.

Alone in the room with the drained, and too exhausted to move, I just stared at Dean. At the line of his profile, his eyelashes resting on his cheeks, as though he were sleeping. He was still so beautiful it made my heart ache, and I longed to see him move, to smile, even to see him cry again.

If the leech died, I never would.

But they still didn't know who the leech was. Working out

it was Terry would be pretty hard unless you knew him. And I was the only one in the whole group who did. Police Captain Terry Pence, working long hours, serving his community. Who would ever have suspected?

I had hope that I still had some time. Time to heal, grow strong again.

Kimmy pounced at the end of my bed, and chirped a high meow. I wriggled my fingers, and she came up to me, curled at my side, and purred loudly as I scratched her chin. She probably wasn't used to her bed companions returning affection. She snuggled up beside me, lulling my senses with her healing purrs.

I was terrified there was no answer, no way to stop Terry. That his powers would grow and grow, leaving bodies behind in his wake. But I was equally terrified of him being discovered, hunted, and assassinated from afar, and losing everyone in this room. For me, for Rayni, and for the Crossmans.

We couldn't give up on them.

I wouldn't.

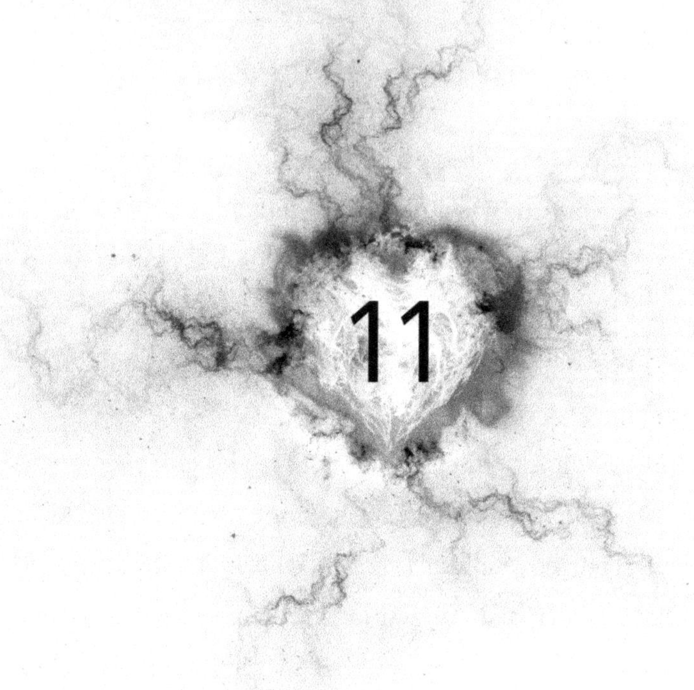

11

Everyone stared at me when I walked into the gym for the afternoon training session. The whole place went silent.

I knew why. I'd seen myself in the mirror while I was putting my training suit on. I'd healed remarkably well in the thirty-odd hours since Terry had beaten me, but I was covered in mottled sickly yellow and purple bruises, with one side of my face still swollen and the cast still on my arm.

Felix had reduced my pain meds and everything felt clearer again, but with the clarity came anxiety. Lying in bed doing nothing made it worse. I could only stare at Dean and weep for so long.

I pretended to ignore the shocked expressions as I moved out onto the mats where everyone had already begun warm-up stretches. The adult empath who ran the class raised an eyebrow at me. He probably knew I wasn't meant to be out of bed yet. But then his phone started ringing and he ducked out into the hallway to answer it.

I took a spot on the floor next to Sway, who winked at me. Rayni was just behind us, and Emma and Bastian were on the other side of the few younger kids. Everyone was in their Limbus suits, and I was glad that training in these was still a thing since two weeks ago, and I hadn't been the only person to show up in a skin-tight bodysuit.

I slowly moved into a leg stretch. Everything ached as I lined my torso up and bent low over my thigh. When I raised back up, Emma and Bastian sat in front of me, and everyone else in the room had stopped stretching.

"Hey," Emma said. She swirled her long, red hair around a finger, and cleared her throat. "I umm … I guess I wanted to say thanks. For saving my life. This time … and last time, too."

She seemed so different to how I'd once known her. Thoughtful, vulnerable—anything but shallow. I smiled with one half of my mouth. "Thanks, for saving mine too, I guess. Figured it was you and Bastian who pressed my panic button for me."

Bastian nodded, his brown ringlets dangling around his sad eyes. "I'm so sorry we couldn't stay. I was certain if we did, he would have drained us. It was intense, knowing what could happen, but knowing it would only be worse if we stayed. Just, whoa, man."

"That man's insane," Emma said. "Seeing what he did to you. I can't believe anyone is that cruel."

"Shoulda seen what he did to my Marigold," Sway said, leaning into the conversation. "But I object to the term insane. I know plenty of sugar-pop insane sweethearts. That man is a *monster*."

Rayni shuffled up closer on my side. "Actually, calling him a monster feels like an understatement."

I frowned. "Wait, wait. You stayed and saw what happened?"

Emma looked at Bastian and shrugged. "Not really. We left a phone to get video before getting to a safe distance. We came back for the phone and to press your panic button before getting clear again."

"You *filmed* it?" I narrowed my eyes. "For, like, a keepsake, or what are we talking about here?"

Bastian tapped his forehead. "I'm not sure exactly, but everything in my senses was telling me I needed to record it. That it was something Emma needed, that would help stop the leech somehow. I can't explain it, and I don't even know if it will amount to anything. My powers—they aren't exactly always accurate."

I snorted. "Like when you freaked out about Emma when you first met?"

Bastian's cheeks went red and he pushed his hair back. "Actually … that one kind of played out pretty much as I saw."

I sat up straight, imbuing my tone with a heavy dose of sarcasm. "Really? You didn't want to be anywhere near her, and now you're both sneaking out for couples' night?"

Sway gasped dramatically beside me then whispered, "Just joshing. I knew these lovebirds have been at it for ages. Can't keep secrets from the queen of institution sneak-abouts."

Bastian gestured between him and Emma. "This *was* why I didn't want to train her. I saw us together. And I saw *her*"—he waved a hand at her fabulousness—"and I felt like that whole concept was not a place that was going to work out well for anyone. But then she insulted me to my face and I figured it was a misreading."

Emma ducked her head, embarrassed. "I was so used to judging people's worth based on appearance. But the environment here …"

"A bit different to high school or a team run by criminal

con artists?" I snarked.

Bastian shrugged. "Hey, I mean, I judged her based on appearance, too. But then she opened up a bit and I saw who she really was. We've got a lot in common under the surface."

Emma crossed her legs and put her hands in her lap in a pose we used for meditation. "Under the surface is somewhere I hadn't looked in a very long time. Because I was worried I was just as ugly on the inside as I'd once felt on the outside. Now, I feel like an idiot for ever letting myself feel ugly, and for the ugly things I did. Because I know it was always my choice."

Sway twitched and scratched her ear. "Self-love propaganda. Don't bully-beat yourself. It's hard to feel good inside when everyone creeps cruelly around you, telling you the opposite."

Emma's bottom lip wobbled. Bastian reached across and held her hand, and she put her other hand on his, and then he joined in with his second hand too, and they both were smiling at each other.

"Uh, okay, enough with the googly eyes," I groaned, but couldn't help the small smile that grew on my face. "And thanks, for not telling the Crossmans who the leech is."

Emma shuffled closer into our circle. "I want you to know I'll do anything I can to help. I want to stop the leech, and get Dean back."

I nodded a thank you, and blinked away tears before they could fall.

Bastian put his arm over Emma's shoulders. "I'm in too. Liv, you saved our lives. We'll keep your secret and anything else you need to save Dean and the others."

"Me too," Rayni said, her voice small. "I want my brother back. We can't let Limbus kill the leech before we get everyone back."

Sway's face was dark. "I want payback for Marigold. But Livvy saved my life too. So I'm in for saving anyone she wants saved."

I sniffled. "That's really sweet, guys, but I have no idea what to do now. I don't have any plan. The leech? He's just too much. What he's capable of—I don't even know how to describe him."

"He's a straight-up psychopath, for starters," Bastian said seriously. "It took me all of one look into him to know."

"Psychopath? He's so good in the community though." *Why in this wild world am I defending him?*

"Actually," Rayni said, "psychopaths often make big efforts to help other people out, to cover their darker urges, or as another way to manipulate people and situations."

"He clearly likes to be in power, and pretending to be the

good guy is a great way to have power," Bastian added.

"Which explains him being"—I glanced from our small group to the few younger kids doing a bad job at eavesdropping—"in his career choice. I can't even imagine the ways he's exploited that. How is he an empath and a psychopath? How can he hurt people so easily?"

Bastian raised his hands palm up. "I can only guess that while his empath powers can absorb emotions, he doesn't actually have them himself. He might be able to label the feelings he absorbs but he doesn't experience emotions like we do, especially compassion. He's an empath without empathy. He can use other people's emotions brutally against them and never feel bad about it."

I shivered. He'd known exactly how to take my love for my parents and turn it against me without so much as blinking. And his arrogance—he didn't want me because he felt anything for me. He probably just wanted to be seen as the great teacher to a student, the master to a thankful slave. He just wanted someone to appreciate his power and make him feel more powerful.

Emma's head hung down, her face curtained by her red hair. "I hate that I used to do that too. Use my proesthian powers to get whatever I wanted."

I shook my head. "The difference is you're here, doing the

work to be better. You're changing. He will never understand what he's doing is wrong. He's a predator, and there isn't a single person he doesn't consider prey."

Rayni bit her lip and looked up at me. "Livvy? I think it would help us to understand all of this more if you told us how draining works. How you did it. We know you didn't know what you were doing at the time, but if you told us maybe it could help us understand what the leech can do, and how we can stop him."

I took a deep breath. "It was horrible. Like being so desolate and devastated that I wanted to let go of all control and consume everything around me. I thought Dean was dead and I just turned into a black hole."

Emma put her hands over her mouth and leaned into Bastian. "I'm so sorry."

I shrugged. "That was ... that specific situation though. The more I've thought about it, the more I've realized it's like opening up the inlet taps of your powers fully. To soak in every single emotion, every bit of energy that the other person has. As empaths, we absorb emotional energy on a regular basis, but just small amounts. When you drain someone, you take everything."

Bastian straightened up with a concerned look under his furrowed brow. "You don't think, in theory then, that it could be done to normal people too? Not just empaths?"

I shrugged. "I guess. Only they would just be losing emotions and not powers."

Bastian's eyes went wide and he started tapping on the suit's screen on his wrist. He held it up, showing us a news article. "Maybe something like this? Tuesday evening, authorities were called to the scene of a major gas leak in the Bellscroft area. Twenty people were found unconscious and have yet to be revived," he read aloud. "But they don't know where the gas came from."

"You think it's the leech going after normal people? Like, maybe a bunch of normal people might equal the power boost of one empath?" My chest grew cold and I wrapped my arms around my shoulders, wishing they were Dean's arms and starting to lose hope they ever would be. "Maybe the Crossmans are right. Maybe the best thing at this point is to end this. He's just too dangerous."

Rayni grabbed me with both her hands. "No! We can't. We have to get Ash back. We can't abandon him."

I squeezed my arms tighter. "I don't want to abandon any of them. But I don't have a plan. I don't know what else we can do. I tried draining the leech and it didn't work. Nothing I've tried has worked."

Sway put a hand on my shoulder. "But you didn't have all of us with you then. We can think of something together. Team Emotional Wrecks, remember?"

I laughed softly. "Go team."

"What about you, Bastian?" Rayni asked. "You were there with him; you know what he looks like, what he thinks like. Can your powers see any further into what we could do to beat him?"

Bastian shook his head and sighed. "I wish they worked that way. I really do. I would have to be around him more to read anything else, something I don't think he's going to just let me do."

"Not without draining you and getting your powers for himself." I shuddered at the thought of Terry with elucidist powers. "You really didn't get anything else from that encounter? Anything from his personality to guess what he's going to do next?"

Bastian scrunched his face up in thought. "I mean, if I had to guess, I'd say Terry would come after Limbus next."

Just as he finished his last word, alarms blared through the building.

12

We all stared at each other, not daring to speak or move, as alarms sounded around us. Ada, Cam, and Max shuffled over closer to our group.

"Maybe it's just a drill?" Emma offered.

Gunshots rang out from somewhere in the building.

Ada shrieked and covered her mouth.

We were on our feet instantly.

Shadows moved past the frosted windows in the entry doors to the gym. One of them stopped directly in front of it.

A deep voice bellowed. "Drop the weapon. Get your hands up!"

The sound of the gun hitting the floor echoed from the hallway into the training room. "My name is Vincent Crossman. I'm responsible for this workplace and those in it. You have no reason for this use of force. I want to speak to the officer in charge, and I want to see a warrant."

"You need to come with us," the other voice said. "And we'll use any force necessary."

"Show me your warrant or I'm not going anywhere. I will not move."

There was a rustling sound and the doors shook. Then more sounds of arguing, yelling, and struggling. A gunshot boomed, making us all duck to the ground.

Following the shot was a thud, the sound of a body hitting the floor. Blood seeped under the door and Bastian moved back, fear on his face.

Rayni grabbed my arm and slapped her hand over her mouth, whimpering quietly. More shouting came from outside. Another loud bang echoed out from the other side door. Seconds passed in stillness, only the suppressed crying from Ada breaking the silence. Then the door burst open.

We all jumped, Emma, Bastian and I moving to the front of the smaller kids.

Dr. Crossman stood there, panting heavily, holding a handgun in both hands, her finger on the trigger. Behind her on the floor, blood pooled and spread. Lying to the side, surrounded by that red ooze were two pairs of feet—Mr. Crossman's, and a uniformed cop's. I swallowed with a dry mouth. *Were they ... dead?* Dr. Crossman's face was ice pale and a spatter of blood flecked her white suit-dress. She did a quick headcount of the room. "You're all here, all okay. Thank God."

Rayni squeaked, "What's happening? Is Mr. Crossman—?"

Dr. Crossman gave a single sharp shake of her head. "No time. We have to move. Police are attacking the building; it's madness."

"It's the leech." I swallowed hard. I couldn't keep the secret any longer, not while Limbus agents, while Mr. Crossman, died around me. "He's the police captain in Bellscroft. I'm sure this is him, controlling these cops."

She inhaled audibly. "If he knows about Limbus ... we have to get you all out of here. There's a team of agents trying to hold off the police. I have to go and tell them what's happening. We may have a chance to catch the leech, but you kids have to be safe. Bastian, I'm trusting you to get them out of the building. Now."

"But we can fight," Cam said, stepping forward.

Emma nodded. "We want to help stop the leech."

Dr. Crossman looked from her to Bastian and me. "You're helping by getting the kids to safety. Even that is a more massive responsibility than I want to put on you, but I don't have any other option right now." Her eyes drifted down to the ground, to her husband's still body. Her expression glazed over, then she snapped out of it, looking back up at us. "I'm trusting you to do it. The kids need you. They can't face the leech. Just look at Livvy."

Everyone turned, and stared. My skin prickled, the ebbing pain of my bruises clear proof of the leech's powers.

"If you don't succeed, that's the *best* outcome you can hope for. And I'm sure you all know the worst." She checked her gun, then stepped back to look down the hallway. "I have to go. Stick together. Play it smart. Be careful. Quickly now, while it's clear."

Bastian nodded. Emma too.

"Let's go," I said. I took Rayni's hand in one of mine, and Cam's in the other. Bastian took Max and Emma paired with Ada. Dr. Crossman nodded to us and ran off to the left. We stepped out of the gym and ran right.

I made every effort to turn my head, and those of the children, away from the bodies behind us. We dashed toward the elevators. Sway ran behind me, crying "Insides should not be out!" over and over again. Emma, Sway, and I had the ability to move the fastest, and the three younger kids were all proesthians too, and did a good job at keeping up. The slick fabric of the suits reduced our friction and we sped faster.

I hit the emergency door shoulder-first, barreling through it. Concrete stairs led up and down, the path splitting before us. Rayni stopped, digging her feet in like a mule and staring upwards.

"We're not leaving without them," she said, and I knew exactly who she meant because my heart was dragging me up the stairs too. "We have to take them with us."

Bastian breathed heavily. "We can try and get them down the stairs, but you'd have to carry them." He pointed to Emma, Sway, and me.

"We can help; we're strong enough," Ada declared.

"Safest to stick together, too," Sway added.

Bastian looked over us all, focusing his powers. "Go and get whoever you can carry out. You get *one trip*, that's it. I'll get transport lined up out back."

"On your own?" Emma squeaked. "I should go with you."

I counted in my head. "Emma, we need you. Even with all of us, someone will still have to carry two people to get everyone out in one trip."

Rayni looked crushed, and I knew she was wishing she had proesthian powers too. "I'm going for my brother. I have to."

Bastian nodded. "I know you do. Don't worry. I'll be okay."

I squeezed Rayni's hand, then lifted and swung her around onto my back. Looking at the three younger kids, I said, "Keep up, okay?"

"No problem." Cam shivered, but his face was determined.

I bolted up the stairs. I held onto Rayni's legs and she hugged tightly to the back of my neck. The three other kids were right behind us, with Sway bringing up the rear. Emma dashed ahead of me, opening the door as we reached the next floor up where the ward was. The stairwell was the one Sway and I had once snuck out of, that opened up right outside the ward.

I came to a skidding stop at the double doors. Felix stood to the side, his uneven eyes panicked. He put his finger to his lips and pointed inside.

I peeked in through the windows and Rayni did too, over my shoulder. She gasped and pushed off my back, landing on her feet.

There was an officer standing next to the first bed in the ward. Ash's bed. Lifting Ash out from under the covers.

Before I realized what she was doing, Rayni had slammed her fist to the button, swinging the doors open. "Get your hands off my brother!"

The man's face was dazed and slightly confused. He dropped Ash, who fell back in a rag-doll slump on the mattress. The cop reached for his gun.

Rayni put her hands up in the air, but not in surrender. Her teeth clenched together and her nose wrinkled, and the sheer waves of negative emotion streaming from her brought tears to my eyes.

The officer's face crumpled and his legs buckled. He wailed in grief, clawing at his hair and face.

"Rayni, stop," I breathed, barely believing the power she had over him, this sweet girl who had pushed happy, calming emotions into me before. I'd never seen what she could do with negativity.

The man smashed his forehead with both fists. His arms stilled for a moment, then, shaking, he reached again toward his holster. He took the pistol in his hand, struggling as he tilted it up toward his temple, desperate to stop the anguish.

Rayni's eyes flashed and the air radiated around her. I reached for her arm. "Rayni, stop. This won't make any of it better."

Tears streamed down her face, and she let out a deep breath, releasing her emotional hold over him. "I'm sorry."

The cop dropped the gun and fell down weeping.

"See something new every day in this place," Felix muttered.

"More coming!" Sway hissed, herding the three kids into the ward. Footsteps came from down the end of the hall, and we all ducked inside out of sight.

"They're going to find us, for sure," Cam whined.

My head snapped back toward the cop. The way he looked around wildly, confused, gave me hope. "Hey, hey, get up."

He looked up at me, and around at the other kids. "What's going on? Captain told us this place was a terrorist network, had to bring everyone in by any means. But you're kids. This feels wrong. It's all wrong."

Jackpot. Rayni had knocked Terry's control off him. But I'd never successfully controlled anyone before. "Emma, need you, quick."

She stepped up beside me.

"Tell our friend here that the people he wants are upstairs, right up on level ten. And he needs to get all the police up there right now if he wants to help keep us kids safe, which I'm sure he does."

Emma nodded knowingly, and knelt down low beside the man, using every ounce of charm and suggestion power she had. "You understand?" she finished.

The sounds outside grew closer.

The cop stood, brave and determined. "Got it."

Sway opened the doors for him, slamming them shut right behind as he left.

We all held our breaths as muffled voices came from directly outside. And then footsteps again, going fast, away from us.

I exhaled loudly and looked around the room at the other kids, and the people in beds, and Dean. "Come on. We need to get these people out of here. Felix, help us unhook everyone and then grab whatever you need."

He gave me the thumbs up and got to work. As he took each patient off their monitoring machines, someone was there to scoop them up. Ada, Max, and Cam each managed one of the grown-ups each, and Sway took Holbrook, leading them away.

In the distance, floors up, gunshots sounded again, making us freeze, and then move faster.

"I can take two," Emma said. She had Mr. Kairu, over one shoulder, and reached out her other empty arm.

"You sure?" I had Dean in my arms. Rayni stared desperately between me and Ash, the last remaining. Emma nodded firmly, and I swallowed my heart as I put Dean into her arm and she ran off. Rayni climbed up onto my back again and I lifted her brother in my arms.

I checked around the room, over all the empty beds.

Felix had thrown a bunch of tubing, IV bags, and medication in a cardboard box and was looking around under a cupboard making kissy noises.

"We have to go," I snapped.

"But—"

"Now!" I couldn't carry him too. But when I yelled, he moved surprisingly quickly. I chased along the hall after him, down the stairs, and out the back exit. We arrived just as Emma lay Dean down beside Mr. Kairu in the back of a van. There were two there, each packed with moving and unmoving bodies. Bastian sat in the driver's seat of one, with Sway, the three kids, and their patients. Emma climbed into the driver's seat of the second van.

I lay Ash down next to Dean, and Rayni climbed off my back, stepping carefully around them.

Everyone was piled up horribly. I didn't know how long they'd last without proper medical support. But at least we were out.

Felix dropped his box into the passenger seat next to Bastian. "We following protocol? Know where we're going?"

Bastian nodded.

"See you there." Felix took the passenger seat beside Emma. He reached out the open window and slapped the side of the van. "Go, go, go!"

I stepped up into the van as the engine revved. As I reached to grab the back doors to close them, I looked up at the Limbus building, hopefully not for the last time.

I hoped Dr. Crossman and the agents would do just what we all wanted them to do.

I hoped we'd be returning here soon, triumphant, safe, ready to have our loved ones restored into their bodies where they belonged.

Through a window a few floors up, a shadowed figure stared back down at us. I could feel in my heart that it was Terry, and a deep, uncontrollable anger took over me. I wanted to beat him the way he'd beaten me. I wanted him bruised and bloodied and defeated. I wanted to strangle the life from him, and the only thing stopping me doing so was the lives of my loved ones he held in his grasp.

I slammed the doors on him and those dark, hateful emotions, and we sped away.

Rayni sat on the van floor, squeezed up against the wall, cradling Ash's head. I mirrored her on the other side, holding Dean in my lap. Mr. Kairu, gray-haired and gaunt, lay held between us. We did what we could to protect them from the swerves and bumps of our wild escape.

"I'm sorry about back there, with the policeman," Rayni said in a tiny voice. "I just got so angry."

"It's okay. I understand. I'm angry too. And scared. And just upset in every way. Everything about what Terry has done to me, to us—we can't pretend it doesn't hurt." My eyes remained on Dean, and I pressed a hand to his cool cheek, willing his body to hold on.

"I can't believe Mr. Crossman is dead." Rayni wiped her nose on the sleeve of her black Limbus suit. Her rainbow hair had been in a tight braid at training, but had been pulled loose and tangled somewhere along the way. I wanted to see her back in a bright cardigan, smiling like a prim fairy princess, like she did when I first met her. Before she had seen such horror.

"Me either," I replied.

"I hope Dr. Crossman is okay. I hope she and the other agents made it out. Or that they've already captured the leech."

I closed my eyes, trying to hope the same, but it seemed so impossible. "At least we got everyone from the ward—" I cut off, mouth turning down. *Oh, Kimmy.*

We left Kimmy behind. Somehow it hurt even more, imagining that sweet cat, confused and abandoned in the building. Wandering the empty beds, looking for her sleeping owner. Finding Mr. Crossman where he lay lifeless and bloody. If Terry had taken over the place, I was terrified to think of what casual cruelty could befall a cat which happened to cross his path.

The brakes went on. We all lurched forward like we'd been washed up on shore.

Felix tapped on the cargo barrier. "Everyone stay there. I'll get the keys. Gosh, I hope I remember the code to the lockbox."

He hopped out, and through the front window I saw the other van pulled up beside us in front of a large but unassuming suburban home in a quiet leafy street. It was well kept and a bit old-fashioned, with a wide porch and attic windows.

Felix dashed around the front yard a few times, flitting like a white moth in his lab coat, then the double garage doors opened and Emma drove us in. I could hear the rumble of the other van as it parked beside us and turned off.

A few seconds later, Felix and Emma opened the back for us as the garage doors whined closed.

I placed Dean carefully down and stepped out over him and the others.

"Where are we?" I asked, looking around the tidy garage, neatly stacked with storage tubs and buckets.

"Limbus safe house. About halfway between Bellston Main and Bellscroft. Everyone out," Bastian replied, hopping down from the other van. He opened the back doors of his vehicle and Sway, Ada, Cam, and Max climbed out, looking wide-eyed and bleary. "Our home away from home. Should have everything we need for a while. Food, gear, cash, beds."

"Bathrooms? Man, I need to pee so bad," Sway declared, running through the adjoining door to the house. The other kids followed, muttering about hunting for snacks.

I turned to pick up Dean and bring him in.

"Leave the patients for now," Felix said. He paced behind the closed garage door, pulling cat kibble from his pocket and snacking on it absently.

"Umm, you seem worried," I said.

He crunched a piece and looked up at me, eyes darting while his brain made calculations. "I'm not worried. I'm fully brown-pantsing right now. I don't think we can stay here."

"The safe house isn't safe?" Emma asked.

"Maybe, for a little while. But if the leech gets Dr. Crossman or any of the senior agents, if he thinks to interrogate them before whatever else he does to them, he'll have access to the Limbus system. Then, *whoosh!* Goodbye safe houses." Felix made his hands like a rocket, zooming them away.

Rayni's face looked drained, hollows deep around her red eyes. "Actually, not just safe houses. If he gets access to those files, he will have the details and location of every empath known to Limbus … on Earth. No one will be safe. Nowhere will be safe."

Bastian leaned face-first into the side of a van and groaned.

"Then what do we do? Where do we go?" Emma hugged her arms around herself.

"We stay here for now. We have to hope the leech doesn't

get that far, that the agents can stop him," Felix said. But from the look on his and everyone else's faces, they had just as much hope of that as I did. "But we prepare for the worst. We load up everything we can into the vans, everything we might need. And we keep watch. First sign of trouble and we're out of here."

Emma nodded. "Good plan."

Rayni glanced back at her brother, then at me. "I'll take first watch."

We split up, Emma trailing Bastian to load up the supplies he selected, and me trailing Felix to do the same. Even though I knew Rayni had headed upstairs and was watching the street from one of the attic windows, I still checked between the closed curtains every time I passed a window too. So far, the coast looked clear, but we weren't sure how long it would stay like that.

We dragged some bedding into one van and moved all of the patients into it, looking somewhat more comfortable than they had during our first trip, then used the other van for supplies. We took a quick trip up to a bedroom and Felix unlocked a floor safe filled with cash, which we loaded into the vans. A lot of what we needed was right there in the garage. We went through the storage crates and buckets and found weapons, long-shelf-life food supplies, and even throwaway cell phones. We weren't sure whether Terry had the info or ability to track everyone else's phones yet, so we all took a burner, and connected up our numbers. My own phone was still back at home, a place I wasn't hopeful I could ever go back to. The place my parents were taken from. *Are they still okay? What will Terry do to them now?*

There were some medical supplies there, but Felix grumbled about it not being enough. It was mostly first-aid gear. Quality first-aid gear, but not the machines and medicines needed to maintain more than half a dozen coma patients. Still, we took everything we could.

Emma rounded up the kids, grabbing duffel bags out of the hall closets and loading them with blankets, toiletries, snacks, and anything else they decided they wanted on their way through the house.

Sway returned to the vans with a loaded backpack and what looked like a dozen energy bars stuffed in her shirt. "This place was finger-licking loaded! Want one?"

She offered an apple-flavored ration bar to me and I took it gratefully. I sat down on the back bumper of the van and bit into the crumbly pastry.

Felix hopped from one foot to another, looking more nervous than ever. "We really should get moving soon. I keep expecting leechified marines will burst in when we least expect it, but then I am expecting it, but still, I think I won't have expected it *enough* to stop them bursting in."

Bastian carried a plastic crate over and balanced it on top of the others. "All we need to do now is figure out where we're going to go."

Sway pursed her lips. "Anybody got any ideas? Long-lost cousins who own huge secluded mansions far away?"

Emma handed Bastian a duffel bag and he squeezed it between the crates and the van ceiling. "Well, there are some places Jake used to take us that were pretty secluded and safe, but the nearest one I know is hours away."

"We need to get the patients back onto proper medical support asap." Felix shook his head.

I narrowed my eyes, looking at Sway.

She wriggled her eyebrows back at me. "What?"

"I was just thinking," I said, "we need a big place with medical facilities, and it needs to be somewhere the leech won't suspect. And I think I know where that is. But Sway's not going to like it."

Sway's eyes widened with understanding. "For freaky real? You're going to make me go back there?"

"Sorry." I winced, then explained to the others. "I think

we should go to the institution."

"Didn't it burn down?" Emma asked.

"One building, yeah. And so they cleared out the rest of the place, but there's another whole building there, sitting abandoned. There could still be supplies and things too. If we're halfway to Bellscroft already, it's close."

Felix rubbed his goatee. "That could be ideal."

Sway dragged both palms down her face, whining.

I stood up and gave her a hug. "You'll be fine. You know what you are now. You're with us, one of us, and we're a team, remember?"

"Uh, guys," Rayni said, poking her head in. "Whatever plan you have, I think maybe now would be a good time to implement it. A cop car just did a drive-by."

"Butt biscuits," Felix hissed. "I stopped expecting it!"

Bastian looked faint. "That means … it means the leech got control of Limbus."

My arms were still around Sway, and she squeezed me back tightly. For a moment, she was all that held me up. Terry had won. He had everything. I didn't want to think about what might have happened to Dr. Crossman and the agents who'd tried to face him.

"And it means someone's seen the lights on here, and there

will be more police on the way," Emma said, heading up into the house. "I'll get the kids."

I took a few steps after her, leaning to look out the window onto the street. It was empty again, for now. My tracker watch said it was almost six p.m. but dark clouds made it seem much later at night, and in the distance thunder rolled.

My tracker …

"We have to leave our trackers here!" I dashed back down to the garage, and moments later was joined by Emma and the remaining kids. "If Terry—the leech—is in the system, he could activate them and find us anywhere."

Everyone triple-tapped the fingerprints on their trackers, unlocking them and dropping them to the floor.

Emma started crying. "I can't. I can't take mine off."

Bastian growled. "They still hadn't given you clearance over it? Felix, can you fix this?"

Felix's shoulders slumped. "Not without my computer. It got left behind. I could hack it. Estimate of twenty, thirty minutes though."

Emma's lips tightened. "We don't have that time." She took her left hand and squeezed it in her right hand. She cried out, buckling at the waist as her thumb bones snapped, and the tracker fell loose to the floor. I cried out in sympathy.

"Done," she said, cradling her hand as everyone stared at her with gaping mouths. "But someone else has to drive the second van now."

"What about these?" I asked Felix, holding up my arm with the digital display pad built into the Limbus suits we all wore.

Felix's eyes trailed back from Emma to mine, watering. "No problem. Not activated yet. I mean, they have Wi-Fi, but no GPS or other things the full-function models have. They were supposed to be just for training, never meant for use in the field."

"Okay. Let's move then."

Bastian put his arms around Emma, supporting her over into the passenger seat of the supplies van. Felix took the other driver's seat and I climbed in beside him with Sway, Rayni and the other kids in back with the patients.

The garage door opened out onto the street as a gust of wind made a cloud of dust and leaves dance along the footpath in front of us. Thunder grumbled and grew closer as we floored it out of there.

14

We made short work of the chain-link barriers that had been set up around the burned out Bellscroft Mental Healthcare facility and drove the vans right up to the front door of the only remaining building on the lot still standing.

Everyone pitched in, carefully carrying out the patients and unloading everything inside before Bastian left to get the vans parked in the underground carpark, out of sight. We hadn't seen any police cars following us, and could only hope we'd made it there untraced.

As I carried the last duffel bag inside, I looked back across the leafy courtyard to the blackened and crumbling remains of what was once the main part of the institute. A shiver drove through me as I remembered the crackling flames, my scorching skin, and Marigold, thrown into the fire. I turned away and headed in after the others.

The smaller side building had been filled with admin offices to support the main institute. It had survived mostly untouched, but there was a small layer of fine ash covering every surface, blown across from the blaze.

A quick investigation revealed the building owners had only cleared out the patient files and medicines, then just locked up and left the rest.

We quickly found a larger storeroom filled with machines and things that made Felix groan loud sighs of relief, and his eyes lit up again when we found a room where salvaged hospital beds had been lined up against a wall.

Everyone worked together to clear out the furniture from a large meeting room and set the beds up in there, get the patients into them, and help Felix hook up everything he needed to. He was going to have to rotate some of the machines he didn't have enough of for everyone, but for now, the patients were safe and stabilized.

I held Dean's hand for a few long moments while Felix fussed around by torchlight, muttering about only having enough medical supplies for a few days. I wasn't sure if we'd even last that long before the next attack came, the next tragedy struck. I rubbed my eyes and headed across the hall where everyone else was making camp.

Although we had power back on, we kept the lights off, knowing it wouldn't do for anyone to see lights on in a supposedly abandoned building. One small LED lantern set to low sat on the floor near the door. Ada, Cam, Max, and Rayni had rolled out foam mattresses and sleeping bags in the middle of the break room. Cam and Max sat on one bedroll, hugging each other and crying, and Ada just lay wide-eyed and still, curled into a ball on her side. Bastian and Emma sat together on a two-seater sofa, and Sway paced.

"This place smells like a mixture of burnt cheese and hospital disinfectant," she snarled.

"But it's safe." *I hope. For now.*

"Safer than anywhere out there," Bastian muttered. "I'm pretty sure we're all considered wanted criminals by now. That Terry bastard could have the entire regional police force out looking for us."

I took in a deep breath and rolled my shoulders. I wanted to lay down and sleep, straight on the floor if I had to, even though it was probably only seven at night. "Felix has got the security monitors up and running and is keeping watch, so we will see anyone coming. We've got enough food to last us a few days or so. We just need to hunker down in here."

Rayni sat up on her sleeping bag, arms wrapped around her knees. "Then what? We live here in hiding forever? We can't. We have to do something. We have to stop him."

She was right. We had to do something. Every part of me burned to act, to save Dean and my parents and everyone. I wanted to rip Terry limb from limb, but I was just so defeated. I didn't know where to start.

And everyone in the room was looking to me.

I shook off the morbid hopelessness that had been creeping into my bones, and clenched my teeth, took one big breath, and nodded. "Okay. We need to deal with Terry right flipping now. Otherwise, he's going to drain every empath he can find in the Limbus database. He's already stupidly powerful, and we don't want him getting any more so, or there'll be no where we can hide."

I let them know everything I did about Terry, his life, his character, his strengths.

"What about his weaknesses?" Emma asked. "Things seemed pretty rough for you when you had drained empaths in you. He might be ten times as strong, but wouldn't he be ten times as weak in a way, too?"

"Yeah, okay. So, what weaknesses do proesthians normally have? Nothing is too small or ridiculous. We just need ideas."

"Actually, there are a lot of things that proesthians powers can't tackle," Rayni piped up. "They improve your input senses like vision and hearing a little, but there are many ways to cripple them, like extreme darkness, or smoke."

"Fire was pretty tough to deal with," Sway grumbled.

Bastian added, "Negative emotions like sadness can be debilitating in some situations. Or just the presence of no emotions at all to use."

I tapped my lips, thinking. "Can we do that?"

"What?"

"Get rid of all emotional energy from around the leech?" I directed my question to Rayni. "Like you did for me, back when you guys first kidnapped me?"

Her mouth wobbled. "Maybe. I could try and pull it off, but depending on how many people there were nearby, it would take a lot out of me. The angrier they are to start with, the more it takes to bring them down to a baseline. I could only do it for a short amount of time."

Bastian focused in on both of us, understanding. "You want to get back there, ambush Terry like he did us?"

I nodded. "I doubt he'd be expecting us to hit back so soon. He thinks he's won."

Bastian nodded. "Yeah, I think Rayni can do it. When I was getting the vans, I spotted maybe a dozen cops at Limbus. Rayni's strong; I could see her managing to calm them. But doing that will mean none of you proesthians will have emotions to draw from either. You won't have any powers."

"I know. But we'll have each other. And we have an emogen," I pointed to Rayni, then to Bastian, "and an elucidist. I don't think Terry knows about you guys. Or at least, he won't until he gets done studying the Limbus info banks. I don't think he's ever come across your types before. That's another advantage we have."

"Plus we have these sexy, sweet super-suits!" Sway said, posing with a fist up in the air.

I cracked a smile, but had to admit that the suit made me feel safer and stronger too. Being bulletproof counted for something. "If Rayni can keep any cops in the building calm and out of our way, we'll be taking the leech on as normal people. One middle-aged man versus all of us—it's better odds than trying to take him with his powers. That is, if you still are all in." I looked around the room, and everyone nodded, even Ada, who'd sat up to listen, and Max and Cam, who'd stopped crying.

"Then we do this. Now. We do whatever we can to incapacitate the leech while he's powerless. After that, I'll drain him and restore everyone back to where they belong. Done and dusted," I said.

Everyone got to their feet, ready for action. I didn't want the kids to come, but I could see from the looks on their faces they were determined, and they had proven themselves capable today.

"It's a good plan, but ..." Rayni stuttered. "C-could we do this without you?"

"Without me?" I repeated, confused.

She grimaced. "If something happens to you, we have no way of getting everyone back from the leech. No one else knows how to drain and return people."

"I—" I looked down at my arm, still covered in a cast, and remembered the warning Terry had delivered along with the beating. Next time he saw me, either I joined him, or I was his next victim. But I had to go. I had to face that monster and beat him down. My blood boiled for revenge. "I'm going. And if it looks like we can't take him down, if it looks like he's got me, I will kill him before he can hurt anyone else."

"Are we really at that point?" Emma asked in a small, high voice.

Bastian frowned at me for a long while. "Livvy needs to go. And we will protect her at all costs."

The circle of suited-up empaths in front of me nodded as one.

We were doing this.

I wished I could promise the ache in my heart that we'd succeed.

15

A *moment.*

That was what I needed with Dean. Just a moment to explain to him where I was going, and what we were doing. I doubted he could hear me, or even knew that I was close, but if I didn't say it then, there was a chance I would never say it at all.

I sat on the edge of the padded gurney and rubbed my hand over his. I spoke softly, so those outside couldn't hear. "You're gonna be so mad." It felt like just yesterday that he wrapped his pinky around mine as we stood side by side in the schoolyard. Back when he was being my stalwart hero, keeping the emotions at bay and helping me to find my stability. I smiled, imagining him already frowning at me. "But this has to be done. I think we've got a chance to take Terry down together."

I had to believe we had a chance. But saying it out loud didn't help the sinking feeling inside. I was terrified to go back into that building, to see what had become of those who were left behind trying to fight Terry and his hypnotized police force. Terrified of seeing bodies, like Mr. Crossman's, and the cop Dr. Crossman had killed in return. The sound of those gunshots echoed again in my head.

I sighed, and poked at the cast on my arm. My ulna, which was apparently one of the two bones in the forearm, had been fractured the last time I went head to head with Terry. But I no longer felt any pain. I wriggled my fingers, wanting more freedom of movement, as though every bit would count. I dug my fingers into the plaster, cracking it away.

Emma appeared at the doorway to the makeshift ward. "We're all set."

"Just a minute," I said, then turned back to Dean. "Before I go, I have to tell you two things. The first is, I'm sorry if you wake up one day and I'm not here. And I'm even more sorry if you never wake up."

Tears pooled around my lashes. The thought of never seeing

Dean open his beautiful gray eyes again was too much. "Second thing is, don't worry about the first thing, because I will come back, and when I get back, you'll be back too. We'll be together again, like we should be."

There was a shuffle in the hallway outside. Emma was still there, waiting for me. I grimaced. *Couldn't she just give me a moment?*

"I've got to go," I whispered, leaning over to Dean's cheek. "Get your sleep because I will be back soon to wake you right up. I love you."

I pressed my lips to his cold skin and breathed him in. Letting go of his hand, I hopped down from the bed and headed out the door.

"Everyone's in the van," Emma said, falling in step beside me. She shot me a few sideways glances. "I know you find it hard to talk to me. And I don't blame you for that; I've done some pretty awful things. But I want you to listen."

I said nothing, just kept walking beside her, the rubber soles of our suits nearly silent down the linoleum hall, adding to the eerie quiet of the abandoned building.

"When I was younger, before Jake and everything, I used to get bullied pretty bad. All those hateful emotions used to burrow into me, cut through me. I didn't know I was an empath, which made me feel everything so much more. There was this one guy …" She rubbed her hand around the thumb she'd broken earlier, bending it slowly back and forth as though testing it. "I took one of my dad's fake guns to pull a revenge prank on him. He didn't find it very funny. He attacked me and my powers kicked in for the first time and there was a big accident and … he died."

I frowned, but still didn't reply. I could tell she wasn't finished and I wanted to speed along through whatever point she was trying to make. We reached the front door, and she stopped in front of it, blocking my path.

"That was when I first started feeling bad on the inside as well as the outside. And no amount of cosmetic surgery fixed that. Everything felt horrible inside me, and I used that to justify doing bad things, like I had no choice." Emma tucked her red hair behind one ear, looking through the door windows at the van out the front. Her eyes sparkled, wet with unspent tears. "You and the others, though? You've made me feel like I could be good again. And it's the hardest feeling ever. Because making that choice means it was *always* my choice to be bad."

I fought off a grimace. Was she trying to apologize? Make up somehow? I didn't have the emotional space for her as well as everything else, but I tried to say something helpful in return to keep us moving. "That gun—the one you had at the convention, and at the bank—it was always a fake, wasn't it?" I asked, and she nodded, looking embarrassed. "That was a choice you made. While Jake and the others were literally shooting innocent bystanders, you always chose not to. I think you've always been better than you think you are. I know you've been crushed down, made to feel small. I'm glad you're finding people to help you find yourself and your worth again."

I nodded to her and tried to push past and out the door, lips twitching. I'd dealt enough with her feelings when so many more important things were happening. Emma reached out and took my wrist, turning me toward her. "That's why I wanted to talk to you, to get you to listen. Because I feel like I'm seeing you getting crushed down in every way. I can feel the anger just dripping off you, and that's with you trying to block it. It's like you're going to explode and I'm worried about you."

"You're worried about me?" I choked up, frozen mid-step. *This was about me?*

"I've felt those same vicious emotions, that pain and anger. I know how easy it is to let that darkness in. I don't want to see that happen to you." She pulled me in toward her, and caught unaware, I tumbled into her arms, squeezed by them as unexpected tears spilled from my eyes. "Darkness isn't going to get you what you want."

I wished I could have said she was being ridiculous, but I couldn't. Darkness had been trailing behind me every day since I found Dean. It called for me, beckoned me, and pulled me down into its grasp. It was the feeling that I could be justified in doing anything I had to do to stop Terry. I could even kill him, or anyone who stood between me and getting my revenge. I had been relying on that darkness to keep me going, to have the will to commit to the violence I knew lay ahead, to be able to lead others into the same, and to risk their lives.

I shook my head. Emma was wrong. I needed those feelings to beat Terry.

"Thank you," I told her anyway, as I backed out of her embrace.

Emma wiped her cheek and laughed. "Come on. Let's go defeat the bad guy, then maybe after that, you and I can start over fresh."

There was so much vulnerable hope in her tone then I almost called the whole attack plan off. How could I be leading my friends and some innocent kids into this mad plan?

The darkness whispered back. *Because you have to. You have to be a monster to defeat a monster.*

I steeled myself and smiled. "Ready or not, here we come."

16

A soft rain had blown in. Thunder rumbled in the distance, as though calling us to action. We were all huddled together on the slope of the stormwater drain around the back of Limbus, having used it to sneak up to the building. Rivulets of water ran down the concrete under us and a small creek had formed in the channel below, dragging leaves and old drink cans along.

The suits we all wore seemed to be somewhat waterproof, but my face and hair were slick and cold from the rain. I blinked it out of my eyes as I narrowed them at the building before us. I wanted to get in there and get this over with. I was eager to claw out a victory and return to Dean and wake him up.

"Right, we all know the deal," Bastian whispered, sounding jittery. We had gone over and over our strategy on the drive in. Before that, when we had explained our plan to Felix, he'd told us it was the kind of plan only teenagers with no sense of their own mortality could make, then wished us luck with such solemnity it made me tear up.

"Powers stay up until we find Terry. We're aiming for as few encounters with cops as we can on the way. Once we have Terry in sight, Rayni does her thing and powers get nulled. We rely on training and numbers, and we do whatever we can to take Terry down while Livvy tries to drain him."

Easy peasy. My mouth tasted of acid and I gulped it away. Everyone looked so confident in the plan that it scared me. They all seemed so confident in *me*, and I couldn't shake the feeling I was using them just to get to Terry.

"Terry will still be a fight," I said, almost hoping to scare the others off. "Even without his powers, assume he's still dangerous. He's been a police officer for years, and we can expect him to be armed."

Bastian looked at me long and hard, and I shied away from what he might be reading in my future. But he nodded and said, "We've got some protection from our suits. But we should maybe grab weapons along the way, too."

Weapons sounded good. I wanted to beat the ever-living snot out of Terry. Then, when he couldn't even crawl, I would take his powers and everyone else's that he'd stolen. There were probably far more than I even knew about, than I even knew whether I could contain or not. It was worth the risk to me though. I would do anything to beat him.

Sway put her hand on my shoulder. "How you holding up? You're glowing hot as a jolly red poker."

I nodded. "I'm fine. I'm ready."

Bastian patted me on the back. "Then let's go. We can do this. Let's take Limbus back."

"Hear, hear," Rayni said. She looked a few years younger than normal, with her hair plastered down over her small face.

Everyone nodded and looked to me. Bastian, Emma, Sway, Rayni, Ada, Cam, and Max.

Call it off. Someone's going to get hurt.

I clenched my teeth. *Everyone's going to be hurt if we don't stop Terry.*

I led the way, dashing over to the emergency exit door, and ducking behind a dumpster. Everyone followed close behind. The team was pumped. I could sense their hope, excitement, and fear.

I quietly tried the door. *Unlocked.* I doubted we were just lucky. Terry thought he was a god. What god needed to lock his own doors?

We snuck up through the concrete stairwell, staying quiet, and calm, and unnoticed. I extended my senses out, trying to track any presence around us, trying to find Terry's location.

Sway found him first. "Uh, gross," she said. "That's him, total gangrenous guts."

She took the lead, and we went up a few floors and out into a quiet corridor.

"*Back, back!*" she mouthed, gesturing wildly. I sensed it a moment after her—a couple of people headed our way. We ducked around a corner. Two officers, in ragged uniforms and looking out of sorts, patrolled past us. When they went the other way, we let out our held breaths so simultaneously, it was almost comical.

Sway crept forward down the hall, around a bend, and turned left at an intersection. We all followed.

There was blood on the floor here, a dropped gun there, but thankfully, no other horrors. *Not yet.*

I eyed the gun, but Bastian snatched it up first.

"*In there,*" Sway mouthed when we reached a hardwood door with a shiny brass nameplate. Dr. Crossman's office. I could feel Terry now too. But I could also sense the presence of a half a dozen confounded and conflicted bodies between us and him, and more above and below us, throughout the building. If we could clear some out, it would mean less for Rayni to deal with.

"Ada, Cam, Max," I whispered. "I want you guys to draw the cops away. Let them see you, then just run for it. Lead them in circles, buy us some time, then just get out of here and get back to the van once you're sure you've lost them."

They seemed unsure at first, as though catching onto the fact I wanted them gone too, but agreed silently. The rest of us hid in a supply closet across the hall while the three kids opened the office door. It only took a second for someone to notice them, and the chase was on. The three kids no doubt fed off my fear for their safety, using it to go faster, pursued by stomping, squeaking boots down the corridor.

I was worried Terry would chase them too, and was ready to burst out and get in the way if that happened. But I didn't sense Terry move at all, and now, he was alone. We crept across the hall, quietly opening the door.

Terry sat with his back to us, typing away at the computer.

Rage flared through me, and I almost leaped across the room to smash his face in.

But then Rayni's turn was up, and suddenly everything was calm. No fear, no anger—nothing came from within me or around me. My muscles practically drooped, and had I been capable, I would have been scared at the loss of my powers.

But even without my rage, my powers, I knew what I had to do.

"Go!" I hissed. Emma and Sway ran in first, and I tried to join them but Bastian had my arm grasped tight in his hand.

"No," he said, with disturbing, calm clarity. "Something's wrong."

I ripped out of his hold and snatched a heavy award plaque off a shelf and went after the others … just in time for Terry to rise to his feet and brush off the attacks Emma and Sway tried to land. I was inches from striking his face with the heavy plaque when his hand snapped up and he grabbed me mid-flight.

Sway and Emma tumbled into opposite corners of the office with striking cracks.

Terry held my wrist, squeezing it high in the air, wrenching my body with it. I gasped and cried out, dropping the award. It thudded beneath me. *What's happening?* He still moved so fast. Was still so strong. While none of us had any powers available at all. How?

The drained civilians. Could they be acting like an emotion store inside of him? I didn't know. I couldn't be sure of anything except that he was infinitely stronger than us, and our plan was sure to fail.

Terry swept back his blond hair with one hand, keeping me held in the other. He was wearing a bulletproof vest over his captain's uniform, and blood stained the cuffs of his shirt. He almost sounded disappointed. "I could sense you children approaching from a mile away. And now it's come to this. I told you what would happen."

His body pulsed with energy and it struck out, opening up and feeding, crawling inside me. I felt sick to my stomach, waves of power lashing and dragging at me. Terry was draining me, right there in the middle of the room.

Emma was back on her feet, wobbling as she picked up the office chair and swung it across Terry's back. It bounced right off him. Rayni stood in the doorway, sweat dripping from her furrowed brow, trying futilely to push the emotions from Terry. Sway pummeled him with fists, completely ignored, less of a threat than a mere mosquito.

Bastian stared. Calm. Studying.

There was a pull in my chest that took my breath away and my consciousness was set adrift, floating out. I tried to hold onto it, hold onto myself, but the suctioning whirlpool of darkness before me was too strong. *Terry* was too strong.

Emma screamed something, but I couldn't hear her. For a

moment, I stared over at her through Terry's eyes, then back into my own face, seeing it slacken and pale. Helpless. Sinking out of the world.

A clapping boom rang out, shocking me back into my own body. I blinked as Terry stumbled back a step, still crushing my wrist in his hand, but dropping me onto my feet.

Bastian yelled behind me, "Rayni, stop. They need their powers back, now!"

I turned and saw him aiming the handgun he'd taken at Terry. He squeezed the trigger again and the sound crashed through the small room, pounding in my ears.

Terry stumbled a second time and released his grip on me, clutching at where the bullet had struck. The bulletproof vest blocked each bullet; each shot barely winded him.

Sway ran forward, speeding fast, grabbing me and dragging me out of the office. My powers were coming back too, but my body was still processing what was happening, still swimming back to myself.

"Get out of here, all of you, now!" Bastian yelled, firing off another shot. It hit Terry in the hand where he had been brushing off the previous one and he howled, more in anger than in pain.

"Take Rayni!" Bastian barked at Emma when she hesitated

beside him.

"But what about you?"

Terry gathered himself and began a slow march forward.

Bastian pulled the trigger again. "You have to go without me. Trust me and just go. Now. I'm almost out."

Emma looked between him and Rayni, anguish twisting her features. She snatched Rayni up into her arms, rushing out of the office. Sway supported me into motion and we followed.

Behind us, shot after shot went off.

As we hit the fire-escape door, Bastian pulled the trigger one last time, the gun making nothing more than a clicking sound.

"Go!" he bellowed.

Terry roared. Bastian cried out.

Emma wept and sobbed as she ran down the stairs with Rayni. My head spun, thoughts spinning loose, fading in and out. I tripped, tumbling down one flight, then Sway lifted me entirely.

We were out in the rain again, back down the street to the van where the three kids waited.

Emma's chest convulsed with sobs and the muscles that strained to keep them in check as she got into the driver's seat and sped us away.

Empty-handed. No victory. No one saved.

Nothing but another dreadful loss.

# 17

My head was tilted limply back against the cinder-block wall of the break room, staring at the LED lamp by the door. I avoided the vacant stares of the others. The worn linoleum floor was hard and cold, numbing my body whenever it touched it for too long. I cuddled my knees, and let the numbing effect spread up through my body.

I didn't want to move, to think. I didn't want to feel. I let my emotions grow numb as well, especially the deep yearning to be with Dean. All I desired was to curl up beside him, draw strength from him, as though even in his coma, he had more life in his body than I did right now.

But I couldn't do that. I couldn't face him. Not when I'd promised I'd return and wake him up, and instead had come back with nothing but the burden of another shattering defeat.

As much as I desperately wanted to go to Dean, denying that need was the least punishment I deserved. I was almost surprised I still felt those urges, that I still had love in me after so much darkness had taken root inside.

I wasn't sure how long it had been since we got back. Felix had seen our faces when we came in, seen that Bastian wasn't with us. "I'll keep monitoring the patients and the security," was all he'd said. He'd looked drawn, helpless, as I was sure we all did.

Ada, Max, and Cam had cried themselves to sleep some time ago.

Emma's wrenching sobs from the kitchenette corner had quieted into regular sniffles. Sway and Rayni had slumped onto each other's shoulders along the wall beside me. No one spoke. No one moved. We were paralyzed in grief and surrender. I had no idea if Terry would track us back here, and who he would take from us next, and I wasn't sure anymore if any of us still cared. We were broken, every one of us.

Emma flopped forward from where she leaned in the corner, landing on all fours and slamming the ground with her fists. "I can't believe it happened like that. I can't believe we lost Bastian."

Everyone stared at her with wide, red eyes, as though she'd broken the spell of paralysis on the room.

"I don't know how we went so wrong. We didn't stand a chance." Rayni's voice crackled with emotion.

Sway patted both her hands in a rhythm against the sides of her head. "Perilously pumped-up parasite. Terry, Terry, terrifying. Monster from hell, can't take me. Won't. WON'T!"

Rayni made soft hushing sounds and put her arms around her.

"He was unstoppable, and now? Now he has an elucidist's powers too." Emma whined and pulled at her hair. "What do you think he did with Bastian? With … his body?"

My voice came out hoarse, flat, and unconvincing. "Maybe Bastian's okay. Maybe Terry won't recognize him as an empath, or is keeping him hostage for some reason."

Emma sniffled again, wiping her nose on one of a million used tissues piled around her like clouds. "Let's be real here. I mean, look how Ash was left. Look how Dean was left. That callous bastard has his meal and just leaves the wrapper on the ground."

She got up and paced, and I could feel anger replacing her sadness, shedding off her in waves. "I can't stop thinking about that stupid video."

I squinted at her, confused. "What video?"

"The one Bastian insisted I take of Terry beating the hell out of you in the park that night," Emma replied. "I still don't know why he felt we had to do that. I keep thinking if only I'd worked it out, worked out the reason, it would have been the key to doing whatever needed to be done and everything would be different."

I rolled my head back and forth on the wall behind me. "It's just a video. What do you think it could do? Earn us some getaway cash selling it off to some sadistic sicko?"

"I don't know! But Bastian thought it would be important."

"Then maybe Bastian was wrong," I snapped. Whatever hope she was trying to rouse, I wasn't having it. I'd had enough of hope. Of trying and planning and losing, losing, losing. There was a poisonous glob of depression sludging through my veins, heading straight to my heart.

Everyone went quiet again, and still, and even though I couldn't see it anymore, I imagined the whole room filled with blue like we were deep underwater in an ocean of sadness.

I leaned my head back and scrunched my eyes closed. I felt light and dizzy since almost being drained by Terry, disconnected in the way I had on and off since giving Jake and the others their powers back, but this time I couldn't shake it. It was like I'd been undone from inside of me. *Get a grip,* I ordered myself.

I floated back and forth, seasick with the sensation, rocking in an ocean of grief. I tried to breathe through it as I teetered away from myself, out of control. A rush of sadness and anger pushed me, splashing over the edges of my mind.

I panicked as I fell, spinning wildly around the room. My body remained motionless behind me.

I landed in warmth, another body. I wanted to cry out, but had no body, no mouth of my own. *What is happening?* I looked out through Rayni's eyes at Sway, and then over at my motionless body.

I gasped back into myself. *What was that?*

I snapped my own eyes open, staring at Rayni. She didn't seem to notice what had just happened, and had returned to calming Sway.

I stared at my hands, trying to ground myself. There had been a moment when Terry was draining me when I'd felt as though I looked back at myself through his eyes. Had that been real, too? In those moments, there had been so much panic and chaos I barely knew what was happening. But I had felt something like that—that feeling of being outside myself, but still aware.

After I'd woken them, Jake and the others had said they weren't conscious of anything while they were drained, but maybe something else was happening with me, after everything my powers and body and mind had been through. Maybe I could put myself inside someone else's mind, and still be aware of myself.

And if I could do that, could I control the other person?

I had to try, to send myself out on purpose, to see how much control I had.

I closed my eyes again, sat up a little higher and crossed my legs, untightening my fists. I embraced the sensation of disconnection, letting myself flow away, like I was a trickling waterfall. I set my sights on Rayni a second time, building a sense of her essence in my mind. Her kindness, her cleverness, her bravery. With a rush like a surging wave, I lifted from myself, floated, and landed again within her.

My first instinct was to rush back to my own body again, but I fought it.

I saw what she saw, heard what she heard.

Rayni spoke to Sway, her voice sounding different through her own ears. "I can ease the sadness away for you if you want me to help you calm down."

Sway's face was wet and snotty, and she shook her head

continuously in a hard rhythm. "My feelings are me. Ferociously, ferally, forlorn. Hearts are hard to have, but I want to stay me."

Rayni didn't seem aware of my presence at all. I tried to will her to look over at me, but she didn't. I tried to focus on one of her arms, attempt to make it move. My focus was strong and deliberate, but she didn't shift even an inch. I was nothing but a tourist in her body. I was there, aware of all of myself, my heart, and my feelings that made me *me*, like Sway said, but I couldn't control anything.

My spirit sank, thinking of Dean, of how I hadn't been able to wake him, of how much I loved him and missed him and how nothing seemed to lead to a way to save him.

I felt movement. Rayni pushed herself off the ground without any explanation and walked out of the room, taking me with her. We went across the corridor and into the makeshift ward, and I expected her to sit with Ash, as she often did. But instead, she went right over beside Dean, and placed a hand on his cheek.

The oddness of the sensation, of feeling Dean's skin beneath another person's touch, of Rayni being drawn to him, shocked me back into myself. I inhaled sharply as though breathing myself back in.

My eyes watered, and my whole body tingled.

Rayni shuffled back into the room, a small frown creasing

her forehead.

"Weird," she said.

I tried to show no sign of my racing heartbeat. "You okay, Rayni?"

Her doe eyes flashed over to mine. "Um … yeah. I think. Just not sure why I went in there."

I opened my mouth to tell her what happened, excited by my discovery, by its potential, but I stopped. As puzzle pieces locked together in my head, I started to realize what it could mean, what I might have to do, and that I couldn't tell anyone. "You're probably just overtired," I told Rayni. "Try and get some rest."

She nodded, then went back to sit beside Sway.

Suddenly, everything was clear. Everything that I'd been through, all the emotions, all the clarity and all the fog, had culminated into one huge realization.

These new powers I had meant I could stop Terry, but only with sacrifice.

I couldn't drain Terry from the outside. I couldn't take him with violence, with darkness. Not in an ambush, not with numbers.

But I had a chance to push his stolen powers out *from the inside*, because he wouldn't even know it could happen. I could make him think he'd won. I would be defeated, and drained, and exactly where I needed to be.

I needed to be in Terry. Then I could get him and his powers where they needed to go. *To Dean.*

Terry was strong. Could my love for Dean be stronger?

Would he go to Dean, as Rayni did?

He will. He has to.

I had new hope, a hope that I could use the power of my love to overcome Terry, but I still couldn't let go of the darkness inside me. I still needed it.

Because for my plan to work, I was going to have to do something unthinkable.

18

I bent over the small table next to Dean's bed, scribbling quickly with the pen and paper I'd scrounged up from an abandoned office. I wrote out my message, hoping he would understand, folded it, and tucked it into the front of his blue scrubs shirt, out of sight.

"I'll be back soon. Just remember I am always with you, no matter what happens." I tried not to feel like I was saying goodbye. Leaning over, I kissed him gently on the forehead and smiled as I pulled back. "I love you."

Knowing this could be the last time I looked at Dean with my own eyes almost paralyzed me. But at least even if I didn't, even if we never saw each other again, I would have brought him back, and the rest of the team, and stopped Terry hurting anyone else. And in a way, I would always be with Dean, even if my body wasn't.

Knowing what I had to do next was even harder.

I wasn't sure yet how I was going to get Rayni alone. But I knew it had to be done. Maybe everyone else would be asleep by now. All of this would be a lot easier if Rayni were asleep. I could already imagine her little face staring at me in fear, wondering why I was hurting her.

Walking slowly away from Dean's bed, I let my eyes linger on his face for just one more moment before reaching the door. When I turned away to the hall, Rayni was there in front of me.

My eyes stung. My throat closed up.

"Hey," she said, almost cheerfully compared to before. "I was just coming to find you. You okay?"

I tried to smile, chuckle, brush it off. "As good as could be expected. What did you want?"

"Actually, it's Emma. She's just worked something out; she wanted me to tell you."

I glanced across the room where soft shadows moved against the low light. People were still awake. I tilted my head back. "Sit with me and tell me all about it in here? I want to stay near Dean a bit longer."

Rayni shrugged, and headed into the ward. I closed the door behind her. When I'd gone to get a pen, I saw Felix had fallen asleep in front of the security monitors, so I hoped we'd have the ward to ourselves for a while. For long enough to do what needed to be done.

We sat on a couple of office chairs that had been wheeled in. Rayni had one of the phones from the safe house in her hand, and she looked at me with wide, bright eyes.

"What has Emma worked out?" A small fear twitched in me, worried Emma had somehow discovered my plan.

"The video. She realized what she could do with it. She knew trying to blackmail Terry probably wasn't going to work. But then she had this other idea." Rayni turned the screen of her phone on and held it up for me to see.

It was loaded to a So-Snap account, where the top post was the video, titled 'Bad Cop Beats Up Girl'. It was public, live, and the hits on it were ticking up faster than I could count.

I wasn't sure how I felt about hundreds of thousands of people seeing me get beaten to a pulp. "And this is a good thing?"

"Actually, it could be a great thing," Rayni said, checking the numbers again herself. "The section of video she loaded doesn't really show anything that gives away empath powers.

It just looks like Terry in his uniform, kicking a girl on the ground. It's gone viral crazy fast. She's uploaded it to other accounts too. We figured the more the better."

I wrinkled my forehead. "But why?"

"Well, it's another weakness Terry has—a lack of social media savviness." Rayni's nose scrunched up at her own joke. "So, proesthians have the power to influence and control people, but it's based on attraction and likability, right? So what happens to a proesthian's suggestion powers if everybody in the world hates them?"

My jaw dropped. "No more cops on his side. No more anyone on his side. No matter how much empath power he's stolen, he couldn't possibly overcome that kind of hatred."

Rayni nodded like a pleased teacher. "He'll still be powerful, but he'll be alone."

My eyes shifted, searching. That was good. But I still had to follow through with my plan. This would make it work even better.

I forced myself to grow cold, hard, determined. I took both of Rayni's hands in mine. "I'm glad Emma worked the video out. It will help. But I've also got my own plan. One I have to do alone."

Rayni blinked and looked back up at me. "You know you

don't have to do anything on your own. We're supposed to be a team."

I smiled at her, my lips fading to a frown. "I have to do this. I'm sorry."

It was time. I had to drain Rayni. I had to steal her powers.

Because I couldn't complete my plan alone. I could only push everyone's powers back out of Terry from inside him if I had Rayni's powers too. My plan meant sacrificing myself *and* Rayni, which made it infinitely harder. I knew I was risking her life without her consent, without her knowledge.

But it has to be done. I took in a shivery breath and closed my eyes, envisioning my powers, the dark pit of despair inside me. I opened myself to darkness, and opened my eyes again, focusing in on Rayni.

She looked back at me with confused, innocent eyes, her pastel rainbow hair pale and grey in the dim room. My nose and throat burned.

Come on. Take her powers. You need her emogen powers to do this. It's the only way. Do it.

I held my breath, clenched my teeth, and squeezed her hands in mine.

My plan was nothing without Rayni's powers, but I just couldn't bring myself to do it. I couldn't hurt her like that, violate her like that. I hated the idea of causing her any fear or pain at all.

Emma's words stirred within my memory. *Darkness isn't going to get you what you want.*

Tears flooded my eyes, and I covered my face with my hands as great sobs burst from my mouth.

Rayni's small arms wrapped around me. "Hey, it's okay."

"It's not. You don't understand. I was going to drain you," I gasped out between sobs and sniffles.

She stiffened for a moment, then pulled me in tighter. I could hear tears in the waver of her voice. "Is that what you need? To save everyone?"

My plan felt so risky, so impossible, I wasn't sure I'd save anyone anymore. "I don't know."

Rayni's voice was soft in my ear. "You do know. You wouldn't have even considered draining me if you didn't think it was worth it."

I pulled away from her, looking deep into her dark eyes that knew too much for someone so young. "It was wrong. I was wrong. Nothing is worth doing that to you."

"Tell me the plan, and I'll decide."

I choked back my tears and told her everything. "I can't do it without you, but I can't ask so much from you. I can't promise it will work."

Rayni sat for a moment, processing, chewing her lip. "Actually, the only thing we know for certain is that if we don't try, it won't work. I want to try. To save my brother and everyone else. So, it's okay. You can drain me. I trust you will do everything you can to get me back to my body."

The tears I had choked back broke through my seal and streamed down my face. I pulled her close to me and kissed the top of her head. Maybe we really could do this. Together. With love, and trust, and hope, instead of darkness.

"Thank you, Rayni. You really are an amazing person. If this works, I'll make sure you're the first to get woken up."

She looked around the ward, at all the empty bodies, and my chest ached imagining her that way. But she smiled and said, "It will be really nice to see my brother's smiling face again. Because I'm sure we can do this together." She turned back to me. Her smile faltered, and although she brought it back quickly, it wobbled on her lips. "What do I need to do?"

I reached out and brushed a strand of pastel hair back from her face. "Just close your eyes. You'll be back before you know it."

19

Draining Rayni was still difficult, no matter whether I had her permission, her blessing, or not.

It also felt different. I hadn't done it with darkness, or ravenous grief. I had done it with *love*. I had opened myself to her completely, taking her into me as though bringing her into a protective embrace. That was where I would hold her, keep her safe, until I could put her back where she belonged.

With her body safely tucked in beside her brother's, I made a quick adjustment to my letter to Dean, and set a few final pieces of my plan in place.

I felt strong, more in touch with my powers than ever before.

Rayni's powers alone weren't enough to tip me into unstable territory, and the combination of her emogen abilities with my proesthian ones meshed together, humming inside me.

But I had to test them, to know I could harness those unfamiliar skills to complete the most important mission of my life.

I headed back to the office with the security monitors and gently woke Felix. Where my powers in the past all required absorption, I focused instead on pushing outwards, sending waves of calm to Felix as he yawned from his sleep.

I told him clearly that I had drained Rayni, and I was going alone to the police station to free my parents.

He blinked and nodded to me like I'd told him the weather report predicted a cloudy day. "Righteo then. I should probably tell the others."

He yawned again, shuffling slowly down the hall, floating in a serenity I knew would crash away when I left. Hopefully right in time to rouse the others to action.

I made a run for it. I needed to get as far as I could as quickly as I could. I used my burner phone to call for a ride-share and headed out to meet it a couple of blocks away.

The driver gave me and my outfit some weird looks. I told him I was going home from a superhero-themed fancy-dress party, and he laughed in understanding. It was late now, and the streets were quiet and empty. Headlights created a shimmering glitter in the rain as we made good time getting back to Limbus.

The rain grew heavier, coming down in thick swathes by the time we pulled up in front of the building. Thunder boomed overhead like a warning. I ignored it. I had done everything I could think of to make this work, now I just had to *finish it*. My plan wasn't foolproof, but I had to try, for Dean, for Ash, for Bastian, and for Rayni.

All I had to do now was get in front of Terry and hope he didn't see right through me and my plan. That any powers he had from Bastian wouldn't pick up the subtle distinction between what I wanted, and why I wanted it. Because the truth was that I *wanted* him to drain me, and that was exactly what I wanted him to think.

I paid the driver with cash from the safe house stash, and stepped out into the rain. The plain front of the Limbus building loomed before me, the concrete turned a dark gray from being soaking wet, sickly yellow light shimmering out of the few windows.

I ran up the steps, blinking the hard drops of rain from my eyes. The front door hung crookedly from broken hinges. I took a tentative step inside. There wasn't a single cop in sight, and none I could sense with my powers nearby. No rush of emotion, no yelling, no gunfire. It was absolutely silent except for the patter of driving rain.

I ran my fingers gently over bullet holes in the walls, and found them still warm. It was obvious that something had gone down there between the time we'd escaped our last failed attempt on Terry, and now. Something I was sure had been caused by Emma sharing that video.

Carefully, I walked forward. My boots crackled on broken glass. I stepped over a puddle of blood on the floor. I shuddered. There must be bodies. Where were they? There were adult empath agents from Limbus I still hadn't seen anywhere. Not drained, not dead. Maybe they had realized it was futile trying to fight and gone on the run. But then how did Terry get into the Limbus system? He must have captured at least some of them, and if he had them I was sure he'd have drained them. *What has he done with the bodies?*

What will he do with my body?

At the front desk I paused, whirling around. From the corner of my eye, I caught the shimmer of something reflecting off the flickering lights. Breathing heavily, I stepped forward and looked behind the desk. It was a cop, shot in the neck, dead. His body laid crumpled there as if he had been thrown over the desk during a fight, illuminated with the blue glow of a screen. Acid swirled in my stomach.

The monitor that lit up the grisly scene was paused on a moment in the video where Terry had struck me hard in the face.

I turned away from the body, but the vision had burned into my mind. Was his death on me? Or on Emma for having shared the video? It was clear it had caused Terry to lose control of the police force. Just the sheer hatred for Terry that half the online world was no doubt feeling for him at this point would have affected his abilities, and the few cops who were still under his control must have been shown this video by those who shook off his influence sooner.

It had cleared my path. It had set them free, but there had been a cost. Maybe some, before they got the heck out of this hellhole, had tried to face Terry themselves, and failed.

No. I wouldn't blame myself for every life Terry took. That was all on him, one hundred percent. And soon, I would stop him for good.

I extended my powers again, trying to sense anyone nearby, pushing as hard as I could. *Oh no.* What if Terry had been killed when he lost control of the police? Or if he had disappeared, been forced on the run?

The unmistakable force of Terry's unstable powers drifted

down to me from above. He was still here. Him, and just a few others.

I headed for the stairs and took them three at a time, running toward the center of power like a moth to a flame.

Fear came from nearby, fueling me and sending me faster. *There, just up ahead.* I sped around a corner, and down the hall, then jolted to a stop. A woman in police uniform stumbled out of a doorway in front of me. She wove back and forth, rubbing her head and pulling strands of gray hair loose from what had once been a tight bun.

She held a gun in one hand. The other hand was bloody, matching a huge stain on the front of her shirt. She saw me and froze.

"What's happening here?" Her voice was a plea.

I put my hands up, focusing both mine and Rayni's powers, hoping between the two of them, it would be enough. "You have to leave here. You want to go home and wash the blood off."

She nodded slowly, as though drunk, and started shuffling away.

"You're not going anywhere," Terry snarled. He stepped out of another room up ahead. His blond hair stuck up at all angles and his face was splattered with blood and twisted with fury.

The police officer hesitated, looking from me to him with

fear in her eyes.

"Raise your gun, and shoot the intruder in the leg," Terry commanded.

Her arm raised. The safety clicked off. Tears sparkled on her cheeks.

I kicked back with my powers, struggling against Terry's control. I pushed with everything Rayni had, with the images of Terry beating me, of the body of the officer's fallen companion downstairs. I could see faint glimmers of the force of Terry's power and mine, meeting and swirling around the woman as we pulled back and forth, vying for control. The cop herself stepped back and forth, her eyes falling from me to Terry, again and again, her body shaking, jerking, confused.

"Go, run. Get out of here!" I yelled, putting everything I had into the words.

She took off. She ran and was out of sight before Terry could reestablish dominance of her again.

He squinted at me, more with intrigue than anger.

"That was surprising," he said, rubbing blood off his chin. "I thought for sure you would have forced Officer Jansen there to shoot me. But I forgot you weren't to know Jansen is quite a good shot. That you couldn't have seen like I can see that she could have gotten a shot through." He gestured to his damaged bullet-proof vest and torn up shirt. "In every decision, every emotion, so many details, so many possibilities. It's hard to see the truth. I'm still getting used to these *elucidist* powers."

He rolled the word elucidist off his tongue as though trying it out for the first time, as though it was merely a novelty to have learned of this new type of empath and that he hadn't drained a friend of mine to do so.

"Limbus told me eludicists often get readings wrong, that there are too many variables." I planted the idea in his mind, hoping to throw him off whatever he might be reading on me now as he looked me up and down, eyelids twitching.

He seemed more unstable than ever. How many more empaths had he drained since Dean?

"What I pick up from you now? That is surprising as well. After all you've done, I didn't take you for the type to give up." He moved closer, but slowly, as though suspicious.

"I'm not giving up. I'm making a deal," I replied.

Terry stuttered out a chuckle that edged on evil laughter. "You think you're in a position to bargain? All right, Lollipop. What's this deal you want to make?"

I held my arms out to my sides. "I stop fighting you, just like you read. I give in. You can drain me, but you have to let my parents go, free and unharmed."

A sly grin remained fixed under his wild eyes. "What about all your little empath friends? You're not going to beg for them too?"

"I'm not an idiot. I know you'll go after any empath you can find. I know what power means to you. But you only have my parents because you wanted me, and here I am. They aren't empaths; they have no more value to you."

His nose twitched, and he crossed his arms over his chest. "Smarter than I thought. So the deal is you give up your life for your parents'."

I scoffed. "What life? Spending the rest of my days on the run? Always looking around corners, terrified of you? It's hardly a choice. I would rather my parents be free."

He walked closer and circled around me like a vulture. I let him feel my fear, my worry, my anxiety, and even my anger. There was truth in those emotions, and I needed him to know my sincerity.

He stopped and held his hand out to me, business-like. "It's a deal then."

I shook his hand, not knowing whether he was telling the truth or not. It didn't really matter either. I just needed him to drain me and to do so without suspicion. If he planned to go back on our deal, then it was even better; we'd be going into this with him feeling like he'd won over me in every way.

"Now, keep still," he whispered in a hoarse, deep voice. "This might sting a little."

Okay, Rayni, here we go. Together.

His grip on my handshake tightened until my palm cracked. I winced and cried out, my knees buckling, but his other arm shot out, holding me in place by my shoulder.

A feeling surged through me, like he was ripping the literal soul from the deepest parts of my body. I groaned loudly, my teeth chattering as his powers drew me from my body, tearing shreds loose, stripping me down to nothing. My eyes went wide and my breath caught, allowing no sound to escape my lips.

At the last drop of my powers, my very being rose upward and out of me. He released his grip.

I watched through his eyes as my body hit the ground. *Empty.*

20

The noise was incredible. Without a body, without my own physical self grounding me, everything was feeling, emotion—everything was *sense*. I felt like I was in a bone-dry field before a thunderstorm, except I was the storm. I could feel, smell, and taste it all at once, a thrumming power, the bloody tang of energy, the swirling hurricane of dozens of spirits trapped within one. It was deafening. Drowning.

I reached out tentatively, exploring those spirits. Within the spinning pandemonium I noticed individual essences, like strands of silk tangled into a cocoon. I knew the names of some of those strands, could feel their beings slumbering within that nightmare. One drew me in, cool, calm, and stable. Without my body, my heart could not react, but my love did. I was made of love now, and that love wanted Dean. I wanted to dive deep into the tangle of essences, to be with him, to cling to him like a life-raft. But I had to keep every bit of my focus on my goal, or we would all be lost. I had to hold tight to myself, and to my love, because that was what would save Dean. That was what would make him whole again.

I strayed too far and was thrashed about in the storm, careening up and down with the current, pulled into the dark clouds. I kept my embrace around Rayni strong, keeping her safe. She was still there, her pattern entwined within mine. I hoped she didn't feel any of this.

I could no longer see through Terry's eyes, no longer hear or witness what happened. I fought my way back to the surface, back to consciousness. *I am me. I must stay me. I must stay aware. For Dean. For everyone.*

I rose into awareness. From inside, through dreamlike vision, I saw my body, still and pale, lying at my feet. No, *Terry's* feet. *I am me.*

He knelt beside me, shook me once, then, satisfied, started patting me down. If I still had breath to hold, I would have, but it was the body I'd left that's chest rose and fell automatically without me.

He lifted my limp arm to see the built-in screen in my suit, and checked through it, as I'd hoped he would. I'd also planted clues on the burner phone zipped into my pocket, just to be sure.

I gave him the location where the remaining empaths were hiding. I let him know they were at the institution, because that was where I had to make him go.

We had to get to Dean. All that mattered now was getting to Dean, and remaining *me* until then.

I could feel Terry's gloating triumph. It was sickening but, at the same time, satisfying. He might have thought he was winning, but he was falling right into my hands. I just had to *stay me.*

But the vortex of power dragged at me, pulling me down. I could only hear the chaos of noise, thunderous static like grating screams. My vision grew dim. I glimpsed Terry throwing my body over his shoulder, and then sank away.

What is he going to do with me? The thought drifted through me, calmly, like the final thought I had before falling asleep. I merged with darkness and sound.

That's just my body. I am me. I must stay me!

I tried to build a sense of urgency inside myself, to slap myself into control. I struggled against the sucking void and for a moment I saw again. We were on the road, driving. Not far from the institute. Already? It was only seconds ago we were at Limbus. I'd lost time, completely unaware. I fainted away again as utter terror took hold.

Nothing.

I wasn't me anymore. I wasn't sight, sound, touch, thought. I was only love. Love for my parents. Love for Rayni, Sway, Emma, Bastian, all the Limbus team. Love for Nati. Love for …

Dean.

I reached for him, called for him, focused all of my love on him, and held onto it fiercely.

And then I felt him.

It was like having butterflies in my stomach, only at that point, I barely remembered the concept of having a body. I could have been gone for seconds, or decades. There was no sense of time. Then existence, the world, started coming back. Footsteps, padded down a long hallway, taking me closer. Closer to Dean. Closer to the surface. Closer to *love.*

I broke through again, exploding into consciousness, awareness of my surroundings crashing into me.

I was inside Terry. Terry was inside the institution.

Annoyance spilled like acid through Terry. He was pissed. He prowled up and down the corridors, finding the place quiet and empty. Relief flooded me. My plan to get the others out had worked, but I still knew they could come back at any time. I had to get Terry to Dean, now.

"Where are they all?" Terry looked into the break room, with empty sleeping bags scattered on the floor, then at his watch. It was almost two a.m. I felt the bitter tang of suspicion grow in him.

I overwhelmed it with love. I let loose everything I was made of. My heart filled with hope, the desire to see Dean whole again, the need that drew me to Dean. I made Terry feel it all.

For a long moment, he didn't move. I was terrified I'd failed, that his lack of empathy would mean he wouldn't be drawn to Dean as Rayni had been.

Then he looked over his shoulder, across the hall to the ward where the drained lay. He turned. He walked.

Terry went past each and every empath laying silent and still in their beds. All his victims. He stared down at them with no emotion. There was no guilt for the taking of their lives, no realization that he had done all of it. Instead, there was a void, as if he were looking at inanimate objects and not real, living and breathing human beings.

"What a waste of resources, keeping these useless shells

alive," Terry muttered.

I wish I could punch you from the inside right now.

He moved on, a small sense of confusion within but otherwise oblivious to his destination or the cause of it. I sent out another wave of emotion, pulling him closer and closer to Dean's bed. He flicked the IV bags as he passed by them.

The nearer we got to Dean, the more aware I became. I soared above the chaos, made of love and power. I was me. I was ready.

Terry stopped and looked down.

I looked through his eyes at Dean's calm and sleeping face. So beautiful. *Love. Hope. Need.*

And then, *fear.* It swarmed my being, almost overwhelming me. This was it. I might only have a moment before the others returned, before Terry took control again and left, before he decided to destroy these shells for good.

Okay Rayni, let's do this.

I drew on Rayni's powers and my own. Summoning all my strength, all my love, I directed the hurricane of energy up, up, and out. Straight through me, pushed along by Rayni, down into Dean. I slammed all those powers, all those spirits out of Terry.

They flowed torrentially down into Dean's chest. His body

jolted and shook wildly. The energy kept pouring, filling him to bursting. *You've got this, Dean. You can do this. Please.*

"What? What is happening?" Terry roared. He leaned over and clutched his chest, groaning. Pain laced through him like fire turning to ice as energy rushed out of his body. A small dribble of spit was strung from his mouth and he dropped to his knees, gripping tightly to the railing on the side of the gurney. "No!"

As the last of the stolen powers flowed out, I released my hold, slipping through as well and falling into Dean. The final impression I got from Terry was complete and utter panic, anger, and confusion. Then, for a moment, there was complete freedom, leaving one body and landing in another.

I sank down into Dean. Back into the swarming cacophony of all those energies. But being inside Dean was different to being in Terry. There was love here, and loss. And even the loss had found a place with peace. It held us and soothed us. We drifted, weightless and formless.

The pull to fade away was hard to fight, but I had to stay, had to hold on just a bit longer.

Because now I had to help Dean, and hope he was as strong as I believed he was.

21

slept. Deep, and unaware. Painless. Dreamless. Then a rumbling reverberated through me, bringing consciousness with it. I was moving, surrounded by energy. I fell without warning and as I landed, I unfolded. Connections reset as I awoke, my senses kicking in. I could feel my fingers, my toes, my face, and my heart, ready to explode.

Where am I? The last thing I remember, I was at the train station ...

My eyes shot open and my lungs gasped in air as if I had never breathed before. My body jolted up from the bed and then landed back, uncurling from the sudden exposure to life.

Everything burned. Power buzzed like a swarm of angry wasps trying to sting their way out of me. My vision swam, all blurry light and streaming rainbows.

What is this? I was filled with so much feeling. I struggled to place myself in the present, the room around me completely unfamiliar. I sat up, squinting through the glare at myself. I was in scrubs, on a hospital bed, but this was not hospital. I tried to track my memories to this point, to find sense in the situation. *I was going home to Livvy. The cop she knew met me at the station. He …*

He was the leech! He drained me.

The rattling of the rail on the side of my bed drew my attention downward.

And he's here.

Rising from the ground, the leech staggered, his skin drenched in sweat and a look of fear on his face. Green and orange shimmered around him. There was a pause, a moment of pure silence when the two of us stared at each other. We spoke through our eyes only, his full and wild, mine confused and quiet. Had he given me my powers back? Why?

His hand jerked out and grabbed my throat, squeezing. "Give them back to me!"

I cried out, but not because of his assault. I barely felt it.

Power surged inside me, godlike, unstoppable, unbearable. I felt *everything*.

My body moved stiffly, an un-oiled machine with a super-charged battery, jolting and lurching. I reached up and clutched the leech's hand in mine. His eyes widened as I squeezed, prying it from my neck.

It took almost no effort to push him away, sending him crashing across the room, like brushing off an ant. I had awoken bursting with strength and unanswered questions. I searched the hazy space with my gaze for Livvy, feeling as though she was there, that she must have done this, brought me back somehow, but I couldn't see her. Just the leech, me, and others who were drained lying still in beds around me. Yet I felt anything but alone.

The leech stumbled, regaining his footing. He glared at me, teeth bared. A darkness grew around him, a vibrating energy, dragging against me. I swung off the bed, pulled the IVs from my arms and placed bare feet down onto the cold floor. I stalked toward him, loomed over him, his attempt to drain me forced back by the sheer power pushing against my seams.

I picked the man up into the air by his shirt collar. "What have you done? Where am I?"

He whimpered a laugh. "She tricked me. She did this."

"Livvy? Where is she?" My heart echoed my words.

"Dead, if she's gotten what she deserved!"

What does that mean? The word *dead* sent my head spinning. *She can't be …*

The leech's face was mad, his eyes flickering wildly around the room. My nose wrinkled in disgust. I held so much hatred for this man, this monster, inside me. More hatred than I thought could come from one person, as though it came from many. It blazed out of my every pore. I marched with him in my grasp to the wall and slammed him against it, relishing in the feel of his collarbone cracking under my hand.

He moaned his words out. "That power is mine. And I won't let you keep it."

Terry's hands thrusted upward, slamming into my chest. Again, I felt the burn and tension pulling at everything that I had, the way it felt when he'd first drained me.

Without a thought, I snapped his wrists. His screams echoed through the ward. I let him go and he slid down the wall.

Anger pumped through my veins. Every bit of emotion I had ever repressed and more pummeled through me, directed at the leech.

He had no chance. I could feel it now, how he was so weak and I was so strong. Every bit of power he had stolen—it was all in me somehow. Including my own, which was all I needed.

I stood tall with my hands out and took in a deep breath. I used my blocking ability as Livvy had helped me learn to do, as my love for her had helped me understand. I extended the chill out, cutting off the leech's powers, and shutting him down for good. With the additional energy inside me, it took only seconds.

Lying on the ground, his eyes opened wide and he grabbed at his chest with crippled hands. "No. No. Put it back. Give my powers back to me. I need them!"

"Like you needed all the powers you drained? Needed to take lives?" I growled, my voice hoarse from being unused for so long. "Where is Livvy? What have you done with her?"

He tilted his head back, laughing through tears. "I threw her body away like the trash she was." His face quickly changed to anger and he roared in pain as he grasped for the gun holstered at his belt. But every moment drew out for me in slow motion. I saw everything, moved faster than he could. He felt as strong as a cornered animal, fighting for his way out. I felt more powerful than I ever had before. So powerful that it scared me. I'd had the skills of a blocker, but never the super-abilities of a proesthian, this speed, this strength. I snatched the gun from his hands, flung it behind me, and pushed my hand down on his throat.

He snarled, feral and wild. "I should have ripped what was left of her to pieces!"

"WHERE IS SHE?"

"I'll never tell you!" Terry breathed heavily, his eyes shifting back and forth, spit dripping from his lip.

The normal restraint I had known my whole life snapped like a twig as he licked his lips and laughed. I lifted him up, crushing his windpipe in one hand as I punched him hard in the jaw. His head flew back and then bounced forward, blood dripping from his mouth. He continued to laugh, as if it meant nothing to him, as if pain was something he welcomed. His reaction only made me angrier. I couldn't control the churning emotions within me. So many of them, unfamiliar, overpowering.

I punched him again, and again. Blood splattered and his eyes rolled around in his head. Devastated rage bellowed out of me. My muscles tightened, fury clouding every other sense in my body.

He grumbled and groaned, his eyes already swollen and bruises forming on his cheeks.

As I tightened my grasp around his throat, blocking every chance at breath, bringing the leech to the edge of death, a warm sensation blew through me.

It pushed the anger in my chest down and away. I could feel … I could feel *her*. I could feel that same warmth that Livvy always made me feel when she was close. I let go of the leech, and stumbled back, horrified at my own anger, at my violence.

I hit a bed and leaned against it, grabbing at the front of my shirt. My eyes watered and a lump formed in my throat. *I know where Livvy is. She's here, in me. I can feel her. I can feel her love.*

My head began to spin and I grabbed it. She had somehow done all of this. Driven the powers from the leech into me. All of them, including hers. And now she held me back from committing the unthinkable.

He must have gotten her. I turned and stared at the leech, bleeding and barely conscious, finding that the all-consuming anger I had before was no longer there. In its place was an embracing wrap of love, protecting me, keeping me stable. She was with me, helping stop the emotions rampaging inside me from tearing me limb from limb.

I snatched the tubing from the IV stand beside the bed I'd woken up in and bound the leech's hands together with it, then tied him to the radiator that he was slumped beside. He groaned and snarled at me, but had no fight left in him.

Once I was sure he wasn't going anywhere, I took a moment

to breathe, to sort through what could have happened, how and why. Sweat rolled down my forehead as I stared up at the colorful lights of emotion swirling around me. How long had I been gone?

I wondered where everyone else was, how Terry ended up here with me. Where *here* was. Was everyone else drained? Dead? Was I the last one remaining?

But most of all, if Livvy's spirit was within me, with all the other drained powers, then where was her body, and what was I meant to do next?

22

I felt seasick from the roiling emotions within me. I had spent so much of my life trying to feel nothing, the sheer immensity of feeling made me want to claw my heart out. I tried to block it off, shut it away, deny it, but there was just too much. My hands clutched at my chest, trying to hold myself together.

Something crumpled beneath the thin cotton of my scrubs top. It felt like paper. I reached in and pulled out a folded letter.

Dean, read me! was scrawled on one side in Livvy's handwriting. My heart pounded.

I glanced back at the leech to be sure he wasn't going

anywhere, then unfolded the letter, more confused than ever, and desperately hoping it held answers. Shimmering halos of color swam across my vision, and I blinked and squinted, trying to see the words. My head throbbed.

Dean,

If you are seeing this then the first part of my plan worked! That's the good news. I'll get to the bad news soon.

I know you'll be confused. You've been gone for a while and you've missed so much. But I need your help for the next steps now.

If everything went to plan, you should have every person the leech drained inside you. I can't imagine how it will feel. I'm sorry if it hurts.

But I've seen your heart, how strong you are, how much you have carried in your life. I know you can do this. And I will be helping in every way I can.

Because here's the bad news. For my plan to work, I'm going to be one of the people the leech drained, so I'm in there too …

I clenched my teeth as pain and fear forced a groan up through them. I knew I could feel Livvy with me, and it was true, but the reason why almost shattered me.

I'm sorry. I had to let him drain me. It was my last hope, because beating him from the outside seemed impossible, but I had a chance to do it from the inside.

If you're awake, then I did it, and now we have to do it again. We need to get all those people, all that power, out of you and back where it belongs.

Just in case I'm not able to stay aware of myself, I've written instructions on what to do as best as I can explain below. I'm sorry you're probably waking up alone. I had to send the others away so the leech didn't get them. I hope they will be back soon to help you. I don't know what will happen to the leech if this works. I hope he's not a problem for you.

I looked back over at him again through the curtains of emotional color. He was more awake now, groaning and crying like a child throwing a tantrum, a ball of blue and red energy. He tugged at the tubing binding him to the radiator but it held strong. Disgust both at him and the damage I'd done to him made me shudder and turn away. I looked to the final words on the letter.

Now, let's save everyone, you and me together. Remember, I am inside of you, guiding you. I'll be with you until you get me back to my body too. And if you can't, if something has happened to me for whatever reason, know that I chose this, and it's not your fault. Everything will be okay.

I love you,

Livvy

PS Wake Rayni up first. I promised.

Rayni first? I could have burst into flames. Livvy should be first. I needed to find her, put her back together, but I had no idea where she would be. She hadn't given me any clues in her letter on how to save *her*. I hated the way the letter sounded, as though Livvy didn't expect to come back from this.

I grunted in frustration and glared around the room, furious at the bodies lying there, that they would get to wake up when Livvy was out there, somewhere, alone. When my eyes fell on Rayni, her small face calm and empty, tucked in next to her brother, a sob of emotion escaped my throat. Livvy was right. I had to put all these people back as quickly as I could. I could barely see, barely think, like this. There was a mess inside of me, a mess that made me lightheaded, heavy, and unwell. I had to rid myself of some of this energy before I couldn't take it anymore. And these people deserved to be made whole again.

"Livvy? I don't know if you can hear me ..." I gulped. I hadn't experienced anything the entire time I was drained. It was like lights off, lights on, and nothing in between. But she must still be aware. If she let herself get drained, had some plan, *this* plan that had worked up until now, she must be in there, awake, in some sort of control.

My body still felt my own, to some extent. It didn't move against my wishes. It just felt full to overflowing. But she had been drained by Terry, then from the inside pushed everything out into me. That was some amazing power, but if anyone could do it, it was Livvy. I believed Olivia could do anything. "Livvy, you did it. I'm here to put everyone back in their bodies with you, and then we'll get you back too." I carefully folded the letter back up and put it in my pocket. "I love you."

I held my breath. A clock ticked. Rain splattered on windows. I didn't know if I was expecting a reply of some kind, but I didn't get one.

I moved over close to Rayni and Ash's bed. My chest extended as I filled my lungs with air in deep, cleansing breaths. I had read over Livvy's instructions and was ready to try my hardest to follow them, but as I stood at the bedside, looking down at Rayni, I felt something else taking over.

"Woah," I gasped.

Pressure filled my chest. Light drifted out from my body in a long, bright stream of spinning color. Wisps of energy flowed down over Rayni, lighting up her face as though she glowed from the inside. I waited, staring openmouthed as her pupils moved beneath her eyelids, her lips twitched.

She shot straight up, taking in gasping breaths. First breath, she stared at her hands. Second breath, she turned her head, taking in the whole room. Third breath, she looked up at me, her jaw dropping and tears shimmering in her eyes.

"Livvy did it? She really did it?" Her voice was a high-pitched whisper.

"She did something all right," I said, irrationally jealous that Rayni already seemed to know more about what Livvy was doing than I did.

Then Rayni threw herself into my arms, hugging me tightly. I looked down at her rainbow-topped head and patted her back awkwardly. She shivered against me. "I'm so happy it worked. I tried to be brave about it, but it was pretty scary being drained, even by Livvy."

"Wait, what?"

"It's okay. She needed my powers to push everything out

of the leech. Isn't she here?" Rayni leaned back away from me, looking around the room again. "Did you revive me first?"

I nodded. "Livvy's letter told me to. I don't know where she is."

Rayni mouthed a slow *"oh"* as her eyes flickered back and forth, trying to work things out. "Terry, the leech—he took over Limbus. Livvy said she'd look for him there first, then draw him back here to you, so she's probably still there."

"And where is here?" I asked.

"Bellscroft, at the burned down institute. Part of it, at least."

I breathed in and recognized the ashy smell on the air. We were in Bellscroft, and Livvy was all the way down in Bellston Main. I hated knowing she could be so far away, if she even was where Rayni thought she would be. "We need to get to her," I whispered.

Rayni nodded, a sharp, single nod. "Right. I'm here to help. But I think we need to sort you out first. I can feel all of that energy inside of you. How are you even standing?"

I grunted. "I don't know either. But I have no choice. I have to keep going, get everyone put back in their bodies, and find Livvy. But I still barely understand what's happening."

Rayni grinned wryly. "I'll try and fill you in as best as I can, and I'll do what I can to ease things for you until we get all that power out of you."

She put her hand on my wrist with a smile. Instantly, my muscles relaxed and I felt calm and clear again. "Thank you. Okay, let's wake some people up."

Rayni climbed down off the bed. She wore what looked like a black superhero suit. *I really must have missed a lot.* She wobbled for a moment on her feet, then took up position behind me like she had when Livvy revived Jake and the others. "Okay, are you going to do them all at once like Livvy did, or just one at a time?"

My eyes grew big and I looked around. "I'm not really sure I'm the one making that decision."

"Okay, well, can we try and start with Ash?"

I looked down at her brother's motionless body. He was gaunt compared to how he'd appeared the last time I'd seen him. "Of course."

As though she knew we were ready, Livvy seemed to kick off the process again from within me, and I signaled for Rayni to do her part. I watched the energy flow back into Ash and we both stood there holding our breaths, waiting for him to wake.

Ash's eyes were slower to open than Rayni's, his lungs struggling harder to draw breath … but he woke. He choked on his words, looking around frantically. "The leech, he's, he's …"

"It's okay. It's all okay. You're back." Rayni's cheeks were wet as she flopped onto her brother's chest.

We gave Ash the ten-second recap before leaving him to rest and recover as we continued around the room, reviving empath after empath. I didn't know most of them, but I felt each of their energies, unique and sparkling as it left me, returning to where it belonged.

One by one, they awoke—some confused and terrified, others relieved and thankful. All weak, bodies struggling with their return to life. We needed a doctor, but I couldn't wait any longer to get these powers out of me. Time ticked by, and my impatience grew. It was all taking too long. Way too long. Livvy was out there somewhere and I needed to find her. I needed her.

We reached the final bed where Mr. Kairu lay.

And nothing happened.

"Livvy?" I questioned, but again, there was no form of response, and this time also no help from within. *Liv, are you okay? Don't lose yourself in there.*

There was no way to know what was happening with her, only that every second taken felt like she was slipping away.

After reviving all the others, I had experienced enough, sensed enough, to understand the process. At least I hoped so, as I stepped up to do it without Livvy's help. I knew Mr. Kairu was a blocker, and the last one other than myself left to be returned, so it was easier to separate his energy out than the others.

I signaled Rayni again and we worked together, pushing his essence into his body.

It was done. Every drained empath in the room stirred, coming back to life. I felt a huge relief. That was a lot of energy lifted off my shoulders. I still felt powerful—countless more energies dwelled within me. Rayni told me maybe Bastian had been drained too, and other adult empaths from Limbus, and even civilians. But I already felt more stable.

"How long has it been?" croaked Mr. Kairu, just as other voices filled the hallway behind us, along with a storm of footsteps.

Sway appeared in a flash beside me, also wearing one of those black suits. She was saturated, her face in grim shock. "Oh my good gurgling God. They're awake!"

The whole team piled in right after, crowding the space.

"What on earth?" Emma was there in the super uniform as well, with three younger kids dressed the same, all soaking wet, looking ready for a fight. Their expressions shifted quickly, and the explosion of mixed emotions coming from them almost knocked me off my feet.

Felix pushed through next, took a look at all the moving patients, and started dashing around between them. "Vitals! Vitals! No, don't move! My kingdom for a nurse!"

I recognized Dr. Crossman next. She looked in a bad way, like she'd just crawled out of a minefield. But she stepped over to the patients as well, rolled up her sleeves, and got to work helping Felix check everyone over. "How did this happen?"

I opened my mouth to answer.

"Ray-ray!" Sway yelled over everything else, glomping Rayni and knocking them both back into a bed.

"Dean?"

It took a moment for me to spot the person who'd spoken. My eyes shifted over to the doorway where Livvy's parents stood. They looked scared and wildly angry. Livvy's mom reached a hand toward me. "Oh, Dean. You're back. It's so good to see—"

Her eyes landed on the leech.

Her scream halted all the reunions and questions shooting around the room as everyone took in the man who had been hidden, huddled and still against the radiator he was tied to.

"It's okay. He's blocked; he can't do anything to anyone," I said, wincing away from the tidal wave of fear and anger smashing through my muscles.

"How? What happened here? Where's Livvy?" Emma asked.

"She wasn't at Limbus?" I shot back.

Emma frowned. "I don't know, we weren't there. Last thing we knew, she went nuts and drained Rayni, then took off, saying she was going to the police station to save her parents. We went after her but she wasn't there at all. The whole place was in riot, with Terry losing his control over the cops. We got her parents back, and Dr. Crossman too."

Rayni pushed forward. "Actually, Livvy said she was sending you guys off a different way so you wouldn't be here when the leech was. She had it all planned out, told me everything before I let her drain me."

"What?" half the room seemed to ask at once.

I itched to move. I needed to get going, to find Livvy, but we all needed answers. We took a few minutes to exchange as much information as we all had, and the picture of what had gone down became much clearer.

"So she's still in here somewhere," I finished up my part of the story, tapping my chest. Livvy's parents held each other, hands over their mouths. "But we don't have her body."

Emma put her hands on her hips. "Then we need to go find her! And we need to go fast. The weather is getting crazy out there, and who knows where she's been left by that monster."

She shot a glare at Terry, and he smiled over broken, bloody lips. "I'll never … tell."

"We'll find her. Maybe the others too." Rayni exchanged a knowing look with Emma, who pouted. "There's still time."

The adults in the room looked at each other. Dr. Crossman grabbed a duffel bag and started throwing medical supplies into it. "Okay. Dean and all proesthians with me; Rayni too. We'll go to find the survivors. Felix, stay here and look after this lot. Mr. and Mrs. Mirawi, please stay here too. Help Felix and the others."

Livvy's parents seemed unsure. I could feel they desperately wanted to go and find their daughter, but were still shaking off the fog of having been trapped mentally and physically by Terry for so long. Livvy's mom glared at him with such hatred she glowed a red so bright I could barely look at her. I knew he deserved it and more. And Livvy's parents deserved to have their daughter back.

I stepped forward and wrapped my arms around them both, hoping Livvy felt that embrace as well.

"It's okay," I said. "I'll do everything I can to bring her back."

Mrs. Mirawi squeezed me tight. "I know you will."

23

Rain smashed against the windscreen of the van. Emma drove, speeding along empty late-night roads running with streams of water. Thunder rumbled in the background, and flashes of lightning ricocheted across smothering clouds.

I leaned forward, looking out ahead of us as though it could get us there sooner. The wipers were going as fast as they could, racing my heartbeat. All of us were scared of what we would find back at Limbus. Emma caught me up on as much as she could on the way. I couldn't believe what they had all been through, what Livvy had suffered while I lay drained and useless. I could still hardly believe what she'd done, giving herself up for her crazy plan. We had to find her.

As we drove down the last stretch of road, I saw the Limbus building up ahead. There were no cars parked out front, and no signs of life or movement anywhere.

Emma swung the van to a screeching halt right at the front steps, sending up a wave of water.

We knew our plan. Everyone loaded out straight away, sprinting off as fast as their powers could take them. The three younger kids were to stay with Dr. Crossman, keep her safe and helping prepare the ward for treating incoming survivors. Emma would search the top floors, Sway the middle section, and Ash, who'd insisted on coming, was looking after the first floor. His powers had him healing up fast, but I worried even searching a single floor would be taxing for his body, which had been out of action even longer than mine.

Rayni would stick with me, searching the ground floor and basement. As much as I was probably the strongest right now, I also had so little experience using these powers, which burbled, unstable as a live volcano, inside me. I alternated between blinding speed and fumbling, head-splitting pain. As a whole, I moved as slowly as Rayni, and I needed her powers to manage the swell of emotions. We were the last into the building.

On the way through the lobby, Emma was moving something

behind a desk, out of sight. "Don't come over here," she told Rayni, looking pale and green. "It's a cop. He's dead."

First body found, and found dead, when we had hoped to find survivors to rescue. Emma, Rayni, and I shared the same grim face, and probably the same hope it wasn't the start of a pattern. Emma nodded to me, then sped off to her area. I could hear movement upstairs, pounding feet racing from room to room as the others searched.

Rayni and I continued down the hall toward the offices, then the gym. Holding my breath, I poked my head in each room, but there was no one, dead or alive. Papers and furniture were strewn around, bullet holes and blood splatters marred some walls and floors, and lights flickered, but there were no survivors. No Livvy.

We picked up the pace, racing down the stairs to the basement. Rayni tried to find out how to get all the lights on, but I went ahead, able to see just enough in the dim glow of the computer servers. Nothing.

By the time we got back to the lobby, Ash and Sway were back already, and Emma appeared a second after us. Frowns wrinkled every face and a green glow of fear filled the room.

"Nothing?" I asked, confirming the unspoken.

They all shook their heads, their lips tight.

I paced, frantic. "They have to be somewhere. There have to be bodies. Could he have sent them off somewhere else? He sent Dr. Crossman down to the station for interrogation. Maybe he—"

"Shh!" Sway hissed. "You hear that?"

It was hard to hear anything over the storm lashing the building.

Emma's eyes popped wide as well. "Is that—?"

"Mew! Mew!" Sway shouted, running toward the rear emergency exit.

I threw a look at Emma as she started to move too, hoping for more explanation.

She shrugged. "It sounds like the cat, Kimmy. Sway really liked the cat."

She followed after Sway, and then the rest of us did as well. As we filed out the doorway into the downpour, I had a horrible thought—that the cat would be the only survivor we found.

Rain whipped around us, into my eyes. Water in the storm drain rumbled and gurgled as it ran past behind us.

Sway was down on all fours near a dumpster, sharing mews back and forth with the black and white cat that hid beneath it.

"She won't come out. Keeps hissing at me when I try and pick her up."

The bedraggled cat circled the dumpster wheel, mewing and rubbing against it.

"Omigod," Emma gasped. Her eyes were wide as she pointed to the opposite side of it. "A body!"

We went around, and there were two, piled beside each other behind the bin. Adult Limbus agents in uniform. Emma ducked over quickly, holding their wrists. "Alive!" she yelled over the thunder.

"He wouldn't…" I whispered, realizing what had happened. I felt Ash's eyes on me, but when I looked at him his gaze had followed mine to the hulk of the dumpster. He flipped the lid open.

"He would," Ash replied, the blood draining from his face. "Those two were just the overflow. It's full of bodies!"

Everyone moved quickly, pulling out person after person, checking for life, and rushing the victims back into shelter, to medical care in the ward. Rayni couldn't carry anyone, but managed to lure out Kimmy, and had her held tight in her arms. I climbed right into the dumpster, lifting the victims out and handing them over, checking each face. My heart tightened each time a face wasn't Livvy's.

"No Bastian? Livvy?" Emma came back after her last trip in.

"That's it. It's empty." I climbed out, my whole body felt

on fire from tension. "Where is she? Where did he ..."

He'd run out of room. Livvy would have been the last person he drained.

I squinted against the rain, checking up and down the pavement behind the building, running over to the side of the stormwater channel.

A body lay at the bottom in the muddy, rushing water. It was face up, identity obscured by tangled brown hair.

I put one hand back and slid down the concrete slope on my heels. I landed in the knee-deep water. The current ran fast, white rapids building around caught up trash and debris, tripping me and tugging at my every step as I splashed toward the black-clad body.

A roar came from upstream. A huge wave of floodwater approached, racing me. It rushed past, pushing and tumbling around me. I lunged, trying to catch the body. The water caught them first and they bobbed up and down on the murky surface. I tried to move with the tide but it was too fast and the body washed into a tunnel downstream.

"No!" I screamed. I was almost pulled under into the current as well.

Emma splashed down into the edge of the channel beside me, grabbing my arm and steadying me in the stream. The others moved around the edge up top, watching.

"That could have been anyone," she said, but it wasn't of any comfort.

The concrete drain tunnel was waist-high, and the water reached three-quarters of the way to the top of it now, and rising. The force of the flooding water was incredible, and everything from tufts of grass to old bike wheels swirled in it. I stepped through, gauging my strength against the water's. The thin material of my scrubs clung and twisted around me, soaking wet.

"I'm going in," I said. "We need to get that person out. Maybe they are okay, stuck in part of the tunnel. I can go in and look for them."

Emma pulled back on my arm. "That's crazy. Do you know how dangerous it would be in there? What if the current gets you?"

I shook her off. "I've got this. I'm conscious, but whoever is in there isn't. There's still some breathing space but there won't be much longer. I have to get in there."

"At least take this so you can see." Emma pressed some controls on the screen built into the wrist of her suit and it lit up bright like a flashlight. Then, using a combination of her teeth and brute strength, she ripped through the tough material of her suit and pulled the screen off and handed it to me.

"Thanks." I took the light, ducking down neck-deep into the water, bracing myself at the entrance of the tunnel as the current tried to pull me in, and down. Emma was right, the water was moving really fast, but that wasn't going to stop me. I needed to get to Livvy. I needed to find her. And if she was the one in that tunnel, she only had a little time to be rescued, if any at all. Unconscious, she would surely drown.

"What's he doing?" Ash yelled. He circled around in front of us, above where the water disappeared underground.

"He's going in!" Emma yelled back.

I gripped the top of the tunnel and took a deep breath.

"Wait! Dean, wait. Over here!" Sway shouted from somewhere.

Ash disappeared from view above us, then he called back, "It's washed the body over here. We can see it through a grate."

I climbed on all fours, up the slope in a flash of speed. Emma and I reached the top at the same time, and saw the others surrounding a large steel grill.

Sway had a thin arm squeezed through, reaching down and holding something up, keeping it from being dragged down and away again. Pressed against the grate was a body. I could see flesh but couldn't make out who it was. A whirlpool of floodwater flowed through the chamber beneath the grate.

The level was rising higher and higher.

"It's bolted into the concrete." Ash frowned at me.

I strained against the metal with both hands. I pulled with every bit of strength I could drag in from the powers within me, from the anger we all held inside us at how these victims had been left, discarded like rubbish.

Concrete shifted, small cracks formed.

"Come on, open!" I yelled at the grate.

Everyone reached in, joining me, hooking their fingers through the metal squares. We braced our feet firmly into the mud that burbled out of the grate beneath us.

"On three, everyone give it all you've got," I yelled above the sound of the racing water. "One … two … three!"

With a collective grunt, we pulled. Steel whined and groaned as it bent, and with a loud crunch the grate ripped right out of the concrete setting, throwing chunks into the air. Ash and I held it up as Emma took hold of the body so Sway could get her arm free. Then we threw the grate over to the side.

The body was dragged out onto the concrete, Emma leaning over it. I knelt down beside her.

She looked up, her eyes red with tears lost in the rain. "Bastian. It's Bastian."

I looked down into his face, his normally brown skin so

pale and cold. My lips twisted and I smashed my fists down onto the concrete.

I wanted it to be Livvy.

Ash leaned over Bastian, checking for a pulse. "He's breathing! He's alive. Get him into the ward, quick."

Emma lifted Bastian's large body with effortless strength.

I watched as she disappeared with him inside and felt all my hope disappearing too.

I got back to my feet, pacing and tugging at my drenched hair.

Sway had both hands over her mouth and was hopping from foot to foot, sobbing and laughing and wailing. I felt the same. We'd found a friend. Saved him. But we were still missing someone we all loved.

I shook my head, looking around us. "She's got to be here somewhere."

Ash wiped his white hair off his face. His teeth chattered. "She might not be in there. She was his final victim. She could be anywhere."

I nodded and looked down at the broken drain. There was a ton of debris collecting at the lip, spilling over it. Twigs, leaves, and small branches pushed through the paper and plastic trash, creating a cover over the muddy water. I shook my head, turning away.

Something caught my eye and I stopped. Disbelief froze me for mere micro-seconds. Then I landed on my knees in the mud, raking through the flotsam with clawed hands.

"Fingertips," I shouted at Ash. "Someone else is in there."

I couldn't reach far enough, the water swirling and dragging away whoever was there. I jumped down into the filled chamber, chin deep, holding onto the top edge with one hand and reaching down as far as I could with the other, finding human flesh. I grabbed onto it, pulling hard. "Get us out!"

Ash and Sway reached in, grabbed me under the armpits and pulled against the sucking water, sending me and the body flying up and out of the drain.

I fell back into the mud and muck.

Livvy landed right on top of me.

"Livvy?" I gasped. I grabbed her face and tilted it up toward mine, wiping pieces of stuck leaves and the tangle of hair off of her. "Hold on. Hold on. I've got you."

She was ice cold. I pressed my fingers to her neck. My hands clattered and I couldn't feel anything outside of the rampage of my own heart and emotions.

There seemed to be no signs of life from her at all.

The next moments skipped in time with my thundering heart. *Thu-thump.* I cradled Livvy tight in my arms. I ran.

Thu-thump. We were in the building, in the ward.

Thu-thump. Dr. Crossman injected something straight into Livvy's chest.

Thu-thump. Rayni watched from the side, clinging to the cat, crying into its fur.

Thu-thump. Defibrillation pads attached to Livvy's bare skin. *Clear.*

Thu-thump. Machines beeped, beeped, buzzed.

Thu-thump. The rainbow of emotions grew so bright, I couldn't see. I was burning out from the inside.

Thu-thump.

"Dean, DEAN!" Dr. Crossman shook me, yelling. "She needs to be back in her body. Her proesthian healing powers, it's her only chance. *Now! Put her back now!*"

24

I've never felt so cold. Too cold to even shiver, I felt like if I opened my frozen eyelids, they would snap.

Warmth teased at my slow, lurching heartbeat, spreading through my veins, connecting me back to my arms and legs, to my face, to my powers. Breath gurgled in my chest. I wheezed, and felt hands on mine, holding tight, squeezing more warmth into me.

"Livvy?" It was Dean's voice, choked with worry.

I'm here, I tried to answer, but I wasn't sure I was, where I was, what I was, other than tired. *So tired.*

"She's stabilizing. You did it."

More voices, muttering, celebrating, crying.

Sound faded in and out. "She'll probably need some time to … Can restore the others … Here when she wakes up."

Everything faded out again.

I felt wrapped in a cocoon of love, joy, and relief. It warmed me as I listened to the sound of my heart growing stronger. Then I heard more familiar voices again, pushing their way into my dreams.

I opened my eyes just a crack, squinting at the real world. Dean leaned over me from one side, and Dr. Crossman from the other. More blurry figures stood behind them. They all looked so pale and drawn that I wondered for a moment if we were all dead, just ghosts now.

Remember. Remember where you are, what happened.

I had been out of my body for so long, through so many other bodies, that everything felt surreal. The last thing I remembered was helping Dean restore people in the institution. No … I remembered a cat, meowing. Maybe rain. Mostly nothingness, big gaps in time and awareness. I had struggled to stay, to remember myself, but even now everything blurred.

"Am I me?" I croaked.

Dean brushed his hand down my cheek. "Welcome back, sleeping beauty."

Still half dreaming, I imagined being trapped in slumber for a hundred years. My eyes popped open wide. "How long, how long was I gone?"

He chuckled, a sound of pure relief. "It's okay. Not long. You've only been back in your body a few hours. But it was in bad shape. You've been resting and healing."

My body—damp and wrapped in blankets and heat pillows. *My* body.

"What happened? After—"

"Is she awake?" It sounded like Emma.

Dean stepped to the side, and I blinked my vision clear to see the ward at Limbus, full of people. The bed I was in was raised into a semi-sitting position, and I could see every other bed in there occupied. Bastian was beside me, and adult agents in the rest, only a couple I recognized. Some were already up, gingerly moving around the room. Sway, Rayni, and Ash sat together, in clean scrubs and warm blankets. Kimmy was cleaning herself at the foot of my bed. Emma was just coming in through the doorway, followed by my mom and dad. Everyone stared back at me.

"We did it? We really did it?" I whispered.

"*You* did it," Dean replied.

Someone started clapping, and soon the entire room erupted in applause. Emotions overwhelmed me and I giggled, and cried, and clung to Dean's arm, and then to my parents when they rushed over to me.

"Mom, Dad! Oh, man, it's so good to see you being yourselves again."

"I went to get them as quick as I could." Emma smiled, shyly.

"Thank you." I smiled back sincerely.

"Oh, honey," Mom cried, wrapping me up in her arms as Dad patted my back and my hair. Mom squeezed me tightly, and I squeaked, and had to push her away, gently. Pain radiated through me, and the bruises, the aches from my encounters with Terry resurfaced. She shifted away, but kept her hands on mine. "Sorry. I was just so worried we'd lost you. I still don't understand half of what's happened. But I'm so happy you're here with us."

Dad shook his head. "I can't believe it was Terry all along. I'm so sorry we didn't know, that we couldn't help."

"Where is he?" I asked, panicked at the sound of his name.

"He's done. I've blocked him permanently. It's over," Dean told me.

"It was a risky plan, what you did, but it worked. You got almost everyone back." Dr. Crossman smiled thinly, and I heard the pain in the word *almost*. I knew she was thinking about her husband, shot during the attack. I even saw a faint shimmer of blue around her. I felt around within myself, checking for any sign of other empaths attached to me, an excess like the last time I was able to see the color of emotions, but it was just me. Maybe my powers were stronger now, after everything.

I stared at her, her skin unmarred and healthy, a glow of strength coming from her. I had the vaguest memory of her, through Dean's eyes, arriving at the institute after being rescued by the others. She'd looked like death warmed over then. I couldn't place my jumbled memories properly in a timeline, but she couldn't have healed this fast since then, not without—I gasped.

"Did Dean unblock you?" I asked her.

She half smiled. "He did. He's done some amazing things while you've been gone."

Dean shrugged. "I figured I should try, since she was pretty beaten up and needing to work so hard for everyone else, I thought it would help if she had her powers back. It ended up being pretty easy. I still have a bit of a power boost. Plus having had the consciousness of the blocker who shut her down in the first place inside me—that probably helped."

"Stop it," I scolded. "You are amazing."

"It has helped," Dr. Crossman said. "I've already been on the phone to the police to start sorting all this mess out. We have a lot of cleaning up to do, and I'm going to need my powers to make sure the leech takes the blame for all of this as he deserves, in a way that makes enough sense to the police and doesn't blow Limbus's cover."

"Sheesh. Have fun with that." I winced.

Her eyes glinted. "You are talking to a reformed con-artist. This will be child's play."

She checked my blood pressure, and seemed happy enough to detach me from the IV lines running down to the back of my hand.

"Hey, can you also get someone to check in on Terry's family?" I asked, as I pressed a cotton ball to the hole left by the needle. "He's got a wife, and two young kids. I saw them, the way he treated them. They've been suffering under control for who knows how long."

Dr. Crossman's forehead wrinkled, and she nodded, patting my hand and leaving me with Dean and my parents.

More people were moving around the room now. Other proesthians—who hadn't been sucked through a stormwater drain and almost drowned—were healed up and heading out, keen to rebuild their lives and home here at Limbus.

"Is it just me, or does your mouth taste like mud and dead leaves?" Bastian called over to me, smacking his lips together. Emma was still picking twigs out of his hair, a look of fondness softening her eyes.

"Our bodies went on an adventure and we missed it all," I replied.

"Pretty glad about that, honestly," he said.

I stretched my arms over my head. I was sore but other than that, I felt great. Seeing Bastian and Emma reunited, Ash and Rayni—it felt amazing to have helped do that. My heart hurt for Sway, knowing her friend Marigold would never come back. But she seemed happy, sitting surrounded by new friends.

I smiled at my parents, then up at Dean. His hair was still damp, and his gray eyes sparkled. "How are you going?" I asked. He had held so much power inside him—I couldn't imagine how that felt. I put a hand to his chest. "What's going on in there now?"

"I've still got more in me than there should be. It's confusing, and sometimes feels overwhelming, but I'm coping." His nose wrinkled, and the rims of his eyes turned red. It was strange, seeing him express emotion so visibly, but I liked it. It made me love him even more.

I pushed myself more upright and wrapped my arms around his waist, pressing my ear to his chest. "I knew you could do it. I knew your heart was big enough to save us all."

25

I paced up and down the hallway at home. *He's late. Why is he late? The last time he was late, things were not good.*

The wall beside me smelled of fresh plaster. It had only just been patched up again from the damage when Terry had thrown me across the dining room and almost right through it. The look on Dad's face when he'd seen it and the state of our house when we'd returned was one of bemused despair. They'd just gotten it back together after the earthquake, and there were all new holes in the walls. I'd apologized profusely for the piles of pizza boxes, and motorbike wheel marks on the floor from when I'd dragged it through the house. My parents had just hugged me, and we'd all worked together to make the house our home again, removing the marks of what we'd suffered through.

Dean had stayed with us for the first few days, but then Limbus had offered him his own place. A small apartment, close to my home and school, on the Limbus budget. We'd talked about it, and decided it would be good for him, and us. I'd miss him being around all the time, but it would feel more normal, which we needed. We could go on normal dates now, be a normal boyfriend and girlfriend, and be told normally by my parents to remember sex safety when I stayed over at his place.

Limbus was helping Dean get back to normal in other ways too, which was what he was doing now. Dr. Crossman had been using her authority and powers to get access to the civilians Terry had leeched, and taken Dean and Rayni to them that afternoon to get the last of the excess energy out of Dean and back to where it belonged, hopefully saving more people at the same time.

He said he'd come over for dinner tonight, and I'd been waiting for him to arrive since an hour before he said he'd be here.

I knew I shouldn't be worried. Terry was gone, powerless and locked away. Dean was safe with powerful friends. But I knew I would always worry about Dean, because I loved him.

And when he got here, he would finally be just him again. Well, just him, and Marigold. Those powers would always be his now, since there was no way to return them to her. He was now both blocker and proesthian. I loved watching him learn to control the new abilities. Now he could match me, speed for speed, strength for strength, heart for heart. He was powerful in every way, and we felt powerful together.

He told me the more he's been opening up, the harder he's been finding it to control his blocker powers. I wasn't particularly sad to see them fade if it meant having Dean be true to himself and his feelings.

My new astral-projection-type powers seemed to be sticking around, but I didn't try and use them. It felt too strange, too risky. I still felt detached sometimes, and more than anything, I just wanted to be me.

Mom popped her head around the top of the stairs. "Dean here yet?"

I checked the time. He was technically only five minutes late. I was about to reply when there was a knock on the door.

I raced to it and threw it open, bouncing on my tiptoes when I saw Dean there, a smile creasing the corners of his eyes, making them sparkle between dark eyelashes.

"Come on in," I said, formally.

"Thanks." He seemed bashful, re-entering the house that had been his home up until a week ago. He closed the door behind him and took a deep breath. "Smells good."

"Dad's making your favorite." I grinned, loving that my parents doted on Dean as much as I did. I started leading him down to the dining room.

Dean smirked and grabbed my waist, pulling me back to him. "I meant you."

I giggled as our lips met. We were broken apart too quickly by another knock at the door.

"Is someone else coming to dinner?" I called out.

Dad replied from the kitchen. "Nope. Can you answer that?"

Mom appeared at the top of the stairs, keeping watch. I could tell she was wary, but trying to appear casual.

I could sense one person behind the door. I rubbed my chest, a serious nervousness flowing through me from them. Looking up, I saw that Dean felt it too, with his new powers.

I opened the door, sure we could face whatever challenge the world threw at us, together.

Standing on the front step was Dean's dad.

I could almost feel the air rush out of Dean. Then I felt his anger build, and then, confusion, compassion, and a wary sense of hope.

I grasped quickly for his hand, and looked between him and his dad.

His dad had opened his mouth to speak, but stopped, frozen, seeing his son there, both of us together.

He looked different. His hair was brushed, his clothes clean, his eyes clear, the redness faded from his cheeks. For the first time, I could see some of Dean in him. Then I realized—he was *sober*.

"What are you doing here?" Dean asked. His tone was more puzzled than aggressive.

His dad cleared his throat. "I came to talk to you, to see you. I wanted to try again, after last time." He looked over at me, eyes creased and apologetic, then down at his feet.

In all the other chaos, I'd forgotten to tell Dean about his dad's previous visit. He'd come by when I was at my lowest point, and I was still ashamed at how I'd treated him. "I'm sorry. I didn't tell you he'd come by a couple of weeks back, when I was home alone."

Dean nodded, knowingly. Mom had approached, standing behind us. She put her hand on my shoulder. "It's okay. You have been pretty busy since then."

Mr. Lasslow nodded. "I have, too. I wanted to let you know,

let Dean know, I've been sober since then, since that day."

Dean looked skeptical. "That's longer than I can ever remember you being sober. At least since Mom died."

Mr. Lasslow flinched like he'd been slapped. "I know. And I'm sorry. I'm so sorry you had to go through that, through her dying, without me being present and there for you."

Dean just listened patiently, his gaze intense. The war of warmth and cold I felt within him made me want to cry and hold him or forcibly make him and his dad hug each other, but I stayed still, letting them get through what they needed to in their own time and way.

His dad's eyes flittered between all of us, too uneasy to hold anyone's attention for too long. "I've had to confront a lot of demons. It's been hard, and I don't even know yet if I can promise I'll stay on track, but I want to. I'm getting help, and I'm trying hard, and … I want to be a family again. Our family was already so broken; I'm sorry I broke it even more." He took a deep breath. "I was hoping, umm, maybe you'd come back home for a while. Keep me company, let me take care of things, ugh, for a while."

Dean stared at him intensely, deep creases between his eyebrows. "I don't think that place is the best for me. Too many memories, mostly bad. I need a fresh start right now."

His father lowered his head and smiled uncomfortably. "Oh. I understand."

Dean's face was blank, but his voice was kind and a new glow of warm love radiated from him. "I think a clean start would be good for both of us. I'm not going back to live with you, but I'd like you to come and move in with me."

Dean's father looked up at him with big eyes. Before he could say anything, Dean continued. "But I have to be clear—if you're moving in with me, you'll be living by my rules. That means you will try as hard as you can to stay sober, and I will try to be understanding of your addiction, and we'll both work hard, together, and with whatever outside help we need too. I want the dad I remember you being so long ago, but I also want more than that. Our home will be one with love, and respect, and we will be open with our emotions, both good and bad. We both need to learn to do that." Dean glanced back at me and nodded. I stared at him with awed, loving eyes. He turned back to his dad. "Can we work together to be a better family than before?"

Dean's father sniffled, shuffling his feet. "I'd like that more than anything."

Tears streamed down my face. "Omigod, hug already, you two!"

They did, in a big, crushing embrace. Over Dean's shoulder, his dad looked at me and said, "Thank you."

I couldn't hold back anymore and wrapped my arms around them as well. Deep gasps of emotion came from both of them, shaking the shared embrace. After a few long minutes we separated, all of us wiping our faces and laughing.

My dad appeared, drying his hands on a dish cloth. "Mr. Lasslow, would you like to stay for dinner? We have plenty. As long as it's okay with everyone?" he said, directing the last question to Dean.

He nodded. "Sounds like a great idea. We've got a lot to catch up on."

26

As my family and Dean's family became closer than ever, I found myself missing my other family—the close friends I'd bonded with at Limbus. I'd seen everyone at Mr. Crossman's funeral, but it was a quiet and somber day. I missed the comradery of training, of fighting side by side, even when the circumstances that made us fight were so terrible. We had become an amazing team, and I missed all of them. Even Emma.

Limbus had put a pause on training for a while as the building was fixed up. Positions in the organization were filled and re-arranged, and people took time to mourn. I was so busy getting my own life back in order, I hadn't even found a spare moment to duck in for a casual visit.

After a few weeks, I received a golden envelope in the mail. A formal invitation to the re-opening of the Bellston Main Limbus building. Dr. Crossman called me personally after that and explained Felix thought a party would be a good idea to bring everyone together again, and to recommence from a place of celebration.

The event was semi-formal, and my parents spoiled me by paying for a sleek red cocktail dress I'd had my eye on from the boutique across the road from Mom's. Strangely, it made me feel as much like a superhero to wear as the Limbus suit did.

I got permission for Nati to come to the party too, and she, Dean, and his dad met us at our place before Mr. Graybiel, the Limbus driver, came to chauffeur us all. I thought it was the first time I'd seen Dean dressed up in more than basic T-shirts or hoodies, and he seemed nervous. But I didn't care what he wore; it was his heart I loved.

We hadn't told Dean's dad all about our powers and what we'd been through right away, but by the time the party rolled around, Dean had trusted him enough to explain. He'd seemed completely awed and humbled, and doubled down his efforts at self-improvement.

At Limbus, they had literally rolled out the red carpet, along with glittering golden streamers and huge bouquets of yellow roses, filling the foyer through to the huge gym room, which had been transformed into a formal gala. Everything seemed back to normal, and I tried to deny my memory showing me reminders of where blood and bodies had once been.

Nati clung to my arm, shimmying her hips. "This is amazing! I feel like a celebrity. I mean, I know it's you who everyone is looking at, but, you know, by extension."

The atmosphere in the gym was hopeful. Tentatively excited, even. Everyone chatted with joyous expressions. Tables were laid out at one end, and the other end was a dance floor. Currently only two people were dancing—Felix, and Mr. Kairu, who held Kimmy in his arms, waltzing with her to the upbeat music.

Ash and Rayni's parents were there, having been overseas during most of the drama. I was surprised to see their mother had white hair too, when I'd assumed the siblings had bleached theirs out. Maybe it was some kind of genetic thing. It was wonderful to see them all back together as a family. Although I couldn't help but wonder what top-secret spy mission they had been on that kept them away from their children during all the drama. And whether that sort of life was the direction mine was going.

I used to dream about romance, and action, and adventure.

And heroes. After all I'd been through, I wasn't sure if it was something I still wanted, now that it felt more possible, more real than ever. Everyone in this place treated me like a hero. In some way or another, I knew empaths and Limbus would always be part of my life, but would I be an agent? A teacher of empaths? A doctor or scientist? Dean and I had both been told we had the option of employment there. But we needed to at least finish high school first, which was all we really wanted to focus on now after all the excitement. We'd been scrambling and studying like mad to catch up. But it felt good, and normal. And I was starting to appreciate normal more than I ever had before.

Mom, Dad, and Mr. Lasslow split off from Nati, Dean, and I to go and mingle with the other adults. We went to find our friends.

On the way, I saw Terry's family.

His wife stood over in one corner, talking shyly to a couple of Limbus agents. She carried her youngest child on her hip, and the other hid behind the skirts of her dress. When Dr. Crossman had checked in on them, it turned out the children were already showing signs of being empaths. Terry's wife had a lot of abuse and trauma to heal from, so I was glad she was getting help from Limbus.

I wriggled my fingers in a wave to her, and she waved back even though she didn't recognize me. One of the agents beside her seemed to explain, and she put a hand to her heart, and I read a 'thank you' on her lips.

We found Sway, wearing a full tuxedo and sitting cross-legged on a grazing table as though she were a centerpiece, chain-snacking and laughing with Rayni, who stood primly in an A-line dress and lemon-yellow cardigan. Emma and Bastian held hands, smiling as they argued about the philosophical ramifications of the final episode of a cartoon from their childhood. Ash sat beside them, and beamed a mega-watt grin when he saw us approach.

I introduced them all to Nati, who greeted them with hugs like she'd known them for years, and then teased Ash about Roxy still pining for him.

"Isn't this fab-u-lous?" Emma exclaimed.

"I know, right?" Nati boomed back.

"And here's the guest of honor." Rayni bowed to me.

I gasped, suddenly terrified. "They aren't going to ask me to make a speech or something, are they?"

Sway picked up a fruit skewer and held it high in the air. "To Livvy! And Kimmy! And Dean! And all the save-the-day heroes!"

"That means to all of us," I said, picking up a skewer too, and tapping it to hers. Then I turned to Nati. "Including honorary empaths." Everyone joined in, tapping fruit skewers, until they somehow went from being stand-in champagne glasses to fencing swords and a couple of mock-fights broke out.

"You know what you guys need?" Nati said. "Superhero code names!"

I laughed. "Rayni, Ash, Sway, Bastian—these guys have supercool hero names already."

"What about you?" Nati pouted.

"Actually, Nati's got a point," Rayni said. "You're a real fair-dinkum hero now, you deserve a superhero name after all your ordeals."

Dean cleared his throat, side-eyeing me. "She's already got a nickname. Her dad always calls her—"

"Don't you dare!" I snapped.

Emma's mouth made an *O* shape. "Omigod, you have to tell us."

Dean grinned slyly. "Lollipop."

Sway squealed, her eyes glittery, then, with all reverence, she whispered, "It's powerfully perfect."

"Super Agent Lollipop!" Rayni crowed.

"You're stuck with it now." Dean laughed.

I punched him in the arm, but I couldn't begrudge him because the sound of his laughter was so beautiful. "What about you, huh?"

"I don't do nicknames," Dean stated, shrugging and leaning against the wall, and no one seemed to want to debate him on it, no matter how much I pleaded for back-up.

"Then Emma needs a name," I huffed.

"I had enough fake names while I was doing that whole criminal thing," Emma said, tucking red hair behind her ear. "I just want to be me for a while."

Bastian kissed her on the cheek, and I stuck my tongue out and made a gross noise. "Just kidding," I said. Grinning, I offered Emma a high five. She slapped my hand back then bounced on the spot, yellow joy radiating from her.

"Team Empaths forever!" Rayni cried. "With our fearless leader, Lollipop!"

I chased her once around the table before giving up.

The music grew louder, and more people moved onto the dance floor. Nati dragged Ash out, and Emma, Bastian, Sway, and Rayni followed. Ada, Cam, and Max were dancing too, and I waved to them. They were such brave kids, and seeing them happy made my heart full.

"You want to dance?" Dean asked.

"Maybe later," I said. "I've got another idea."

I took him by the hand, backing us towards the nearest exit.

My heart pounded and we tried to suppress our giggles as we ran off down the hallway together, checking we weren't seen escaping, relishing in the danger-less excitement. I pressed the elevator button, and as we waited for the door to open, I looked up into Dean's gray eyes, once so emotionless and now filled with joy and hope, fear and desire, mourning and acceptance.

"I love you." I breathed out the words on a kiss.

The doors opened and I pushed Dean into the elevator and against the back wall. He wrapped his arms around me and kissed my neck with his own words. "I love you, too. My hero."

I swooned to his touch and didn't wait until the doors closed behind us before I started unbuttoning his shirt.

Our love swelled and swirled around us, burning like a new star being born.

We were love. We were power. We were each other's, entirely.

Heroes, together.

All my dreams had come true.

A PERSONAL THANK YOU FROM SELINA

Thank you for reading my story, it means a lot to me to be sharing my magical worlds with you. As an indie author, receiving reviews and seeing people talk about my books are like receiving a big warm hug from my readers! Honest reviews help me improve as an author, and help bring my book to the attention of other readers. If you're enjoyed this book, please consider taking two minutes to leave a review at the online store you purchased this book. It really does mean the world to indie authors like me.

If you want to discuss the story or make sure I see your comments, just drop me an email at selina@selinafenech.com. I love to hear from readers, and reply to all personal emails!

SELINA A FENECH
BESHADOWED
DARKNESS UNKNOWN

SELINA A FENECH
BESHADOWED
BLOOD BOUND

SELINA A FENECH
BESHADOWED
SHADOWS AWOKEN

SELINA A FENECH
BESHADOWED
EVERDARK CURSED

MEMORY'S WAKE
SELINA A FENECH

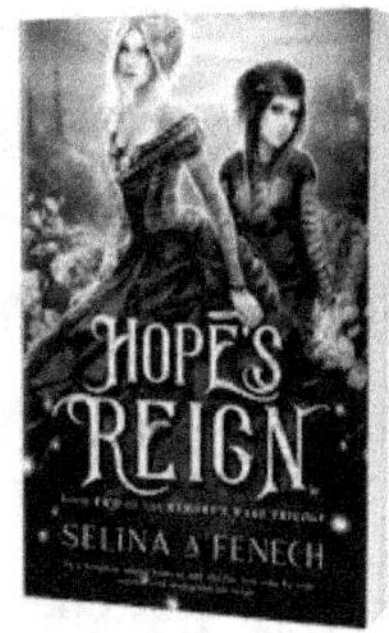

HOPE'S REIGN
SELINA A FENECH

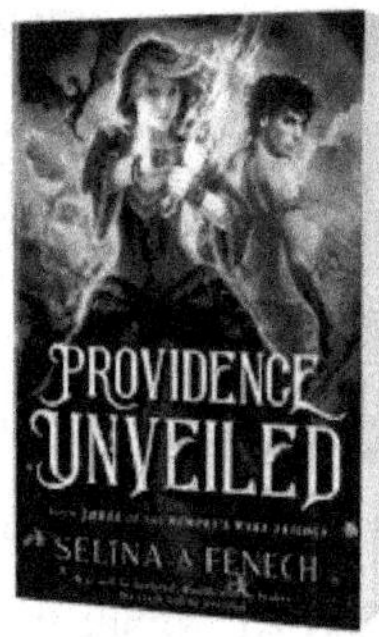

PROVIDENCE UNVEILED
SELINA A FENECH

EMOTIONALLY CHARGED
1
SELINA A FENECH

EMOTIONALLY UNSTABLE
2
SELINA A FENECH

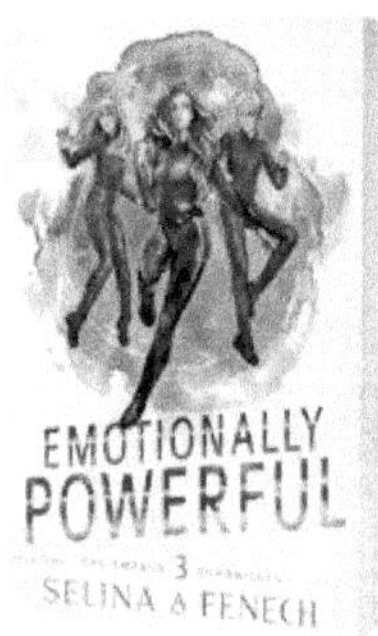

EMOTIONALLY POWERFUL
3
SELINA A FENECH

ABOUT THE AUTHOR

Whether it's painting artworks or writing novels, creating fantasy works is Selina's biggest passion. She lives in Australia with her husband and daughter and loves food, gardening, geekery, and all things fantasy.

Find out more about Selina

Official website www.selinafenech.com

Facebook www.facebook.com/selinafenechart